The Collini Case

Ferdinand von Schirach

Translated from the German by Anthea Bell

W F HOWES LTD

This large print edition published in 2013 by
W F Howes Ltd
Unit 4, Rearsby Business Park, Gaddesby Lane,
Rearsby, Leicester LE7 4YH

1 3 5 7 9 10 8 6 4 2

First published in the United Kingdom in 2012
by Penguin Group

A CIP catalogue record for this book is available
from the British Library

ISBN 978 1 47122 883 4

Typeset by Palimpsest Book Production Limited,
Falkirk, Stirlingshire
Printed and bound by
www.printondemand-worldwide.com of Peterborough, England

We are probably all made for what we do.

Ernest Hemingway

CHAPTER 1

Later, they would all remember it: the floor waiter, the two elderly ladies in the lift, the married couple in the fourth-floor corridor. They said the man was gigantic, and they all mentioned the smell of sweat.

Collini went up to the fourth floor. He checked the numbers. Room 400, the 'Brandenburg Suite'. He knocked.

'Yes?' The man in the doorway was eighty-five years old, but he looked much younger than Collini had expected. Sweat was running down the back of Collini's neck.

'Good evening. Collini from the *Corriere della Sera*.' He mumbled slightly, wondering whether the man was going to ask him for his ID.

'Yes, glad to meet you, come along in. We might as well do the interview here.' The man offered Collini his hand. Collini flinched. He didn't want to touch him. Not yet.

'I'm sweating,' Collini explained, and was angry with himself for saying so; it sounded odd. It's not the sort of thing you would say normally, he thought.

'Yes, very sultry today, it's going to rain soon,' said the old man amiably, although he was wrong about the sultry atmosphere. These rooms were cool; you could hardly hear the air conditioning. They went into the sitting room of the suite: beige carpet, dark wood, large windows, all of it expensive and solid. Collini could see the Brandenburg Gate from the window. It seemed strangely close.

Twenty minutes later the man was dead: four bullets in the back of his head; one had been deflected inside his brain and come out the other side, taking half his face with it. The beige carpet soaked up the blood, a dark outline slowly spreading. Collini put the pistol on the table. He got down on the floor beside the man, stared at the age spots on the backs of his hands. He turned the body over with the toe of his shoe. Suddenly he brought the heel of it down on the dead man's face, looked at him and brought it down again. He couldn't stop, he kept grinding his heel into that face while blood and brain matter spurted over his trouser leg, the carpet, the bedstead. Later, the forensic pathologist couldn't reconstruct the number of times Collini's foot had trodden down as the bones of the dead man's cheeks, jaw, nose and skull cracked under the force of it. Collini didn't stop until the heel of his shoe came off. He sat down on the bed. Sweat was running down his face. His pulse took some time to calm down. He waited until he was breathing regularly again, then stood up, crossed himself, left the room and took the lift down to the ground floor. He was limping, because of the missing heel; the protruding nails scraped over the marble floor. In the lobby he told the young woman at the reception desk to call the police. She asked questions, gesticulating. All Collini said was, 'Room 400. He's dead.' Beside him, the electronic panel in the lobby announced: '23 May 2001, 8 p.m., the Spree Hall: Association of German Engineering Industries'.

He sat down on one of the blue sofas in the lobby. The waiter asked if he could bring him anything; Collini did not reply. He stared at the floor. His footprints could be traced back over the marble paving of the ground floor, in the lift and all the way back to the suite. Collini waited to be arrested. He had waited all his life, and he had held his peace all that time.

CHAPTER 2

'Caspar Leinen here,' on standby duty for legal aid.' The display on his telephone showed a number from the criminal courts.

'Tiergarten District Court, the name's Köhler, I'm an examining magistrate. We have a suspect with no one to represent him. The public prosecutor's office is applying for a warrant to arrest him for murder. How long will you need to get over here?'

'About twenty-five minutes.'

'Good, then I'll have our suspect brought up in forty minutes' time. Come to Room 212.'

Caspar Leinen ended the call. Like many other young defence lawyers, he had put his name down on the legal-aid rota. At weekends they were given mobiles and had to be ready if called upon. The police, the public prosecutor's office and the magistrates had their numbers. If someone was arrested and wanted a lawyer, the authorities could call them. It was the way young defence counsels often got their first briefs.

Leinen had qualified forty-two days earlier. After the second of his two state law examinations he

4

had taken a gap year, travelling around Africa and Europe, mainly staying with old friends from his boarding school. For the last few days his name-plate had been up by the entrance to the building: CASPAR LEINEN, LEGAL ADVISER. He felt it was rather ostentatious, but he liked it all the same. His chambers, two rooms, were at the rear of a building in a side street off the Kurfürstendamm. There was no lift – clients had to climb a narrow staircase – but at least Leinen was his own master, answerable only to himself.

It was Sunday morning and he had been sorting out the office for hours. There were open boxes everywhere, the visitors' chairs came from a flea market, the metal filing cabinet was completely empty. His desk had been a present from his father.

After the magistrate's phone call, Leinen looked around for his jacket. He found it under a pile of books. He took his new robe off the window catch, stuffed it into his briefcase and hurried off. Twenty minutes after the call, he was in the examining magistrate's room.

'I'm Caspar Leinen, good morning. You phoned me.' He was slightly out of breath.

'Ah, from the standby legal-aid roster, right? Good, good. My name's Köhler.' The magistrate stood up to shake hands. About fifty years old, salt-and-pepper jacket, reading glasses. He had an amiable, even absent-minded look about him. But that impression was deceptive.

'The Collini murder case. Do you want a word

with your client? We'll have to wait for the public prosecutor anyway. Senior Public Prosecutor Reimers, the departmental head, is coming himself, even though it's a weekend . . . well, he's probably after a report. So do you want to speak to the man?'

'Yes, please,' said Leinen. For a moment he wondered what could be important enough about this murder for Dr Reimers himself to come, but he forgot any such speculation when the police officer on duty opened a door. Right behind it was a very steep, narrow stone staircase. Prisoners were brought up these stairs from the cells to see the magistrate. A gigantic man was standing on the dimly lit first landing, leaning against the whitewashed wall, almost entirely blocking out the single ceiling light with his head. His wrists were handcuffed behind his back.

The police officer let Leinen through the door and closed it behind him. Leinen was alone with the huge man. 'Hello, my name is Leinen and I'm a lawyer.' There wasn't much space on the landing, and the man was standing too close.

'Fabrizio Collini.' The man gave Leinen only a brief glance. 'I don't need any lawyer.'

'Yes, you do. The law says that in a case like this you have to be defended by a lawyer.'

'I don't want to be defended,' said Collini. His face was gigantic too. Broad chin, mouth just a straight line, prominent forehead. 'I killed the man.'

'Have you already said so to the police?'

'No,' said Collini.

'Then you'd better go on keeping your mouth shut for now. We'll talk when I know more about your file.'

'I don't want to talk.' His voice was deep and sounded foreign.

'Are you Italian?'

'Yes. But I've been living in Germany for thirty-five years.'

'Shall I get in touch with your family?'

Collini didn't look at him. 'I don't have any family.'

'Friends?'

'There's no one.'

'Then let's start now.'

Leinen knocked, the officer opened the door again. Senior Public Prosecutor Reimers was already sitting at the table in the conference room. Leinen briefly introduced himself. The magistrate took a file from the stack in front of him. Collini sat down on a wooden bench behind a low grating, with the police officer beside him.

'Please take those handcuffs off the accused,' said Köhler. The officer undid them. Collini massaged his wrists. Leinen had never seen such enormous hands.

'Good morning, my name is Köhler and I'm the examining magistrate responsible for you today.' He indicated the public prosecutor. 'This is Senior Public Prosecutor Reimers, and you've already met your defence counsel.' He cleared his throat and adopted a matter-of-fact voice; he now spoke in a virtual monotone. 'Fabrizio Collini, you are here today because the public prosecutor's office has applied for a warrant allowing you to be held in custody on a charge of murder. This is the point at which I decide whether to issue that warrant. Do you understand German well enough?'

Collini nodded.

'Please tell me your full name.'

'Fabrizio Maria Collini.'

'When and where were you born?'

'On 26 March 1934, in Campomorone, near Genoa.'

'Nationality?'

'Italian.'

'Present address?'

'Nineteen Taubenstrasse, Böblingen.'

'What is your profession?'

'Toolmaker. I was at the Daimler factory for thirty-four years, ending up as a master toolmaker. I retired four months ago.'

'Thank you.' The magistrate pushed the warrant across the table to Leinen, two pages printed out on red paper. It wasn't signed yet. The contents consisted of the murder squad's report. The magistrate read it out. Fabrizio Collini, said the report, had gone to see Jean-Baptiste Meyer in Suite 400 of the Hotel Adlon and killed him with four shots in the back of the head. He had said nothing so far, but had been identified from his fingerprints on the gun, the bloodstains on his clothing and

8

shoes, traces of powder from the pistol found on his hands, and witness statements.

'Herr Collini, do you understand the charge?'

'Yes.'

'You have the legal right to express your opinion of these charges. If you say nothing, that fact cannot be used against you. You can apply for evidence to be heard, for instance naming witnesses. You may consult a lawyer at any time.'

'I don't want to say anything.'

Leinen still couldn't take his eyes off Collini's hands.

Köhler turned to the secretary taking down the minutes of the interview. 'Please put: "The accused does not want to say anything."' He asked, turning to Leinen, 'Do you, as defence counsel, want to say anything on behalf of the accused?'

'No.' Leinen knew there was no point doing so at the moment.

The magistrate turned his chair towards Collini. 'Herr Collini, I am issuing the warrant that I have just read out for you to be remanded in custody. You now have the opportunity to object to my decision or apply for a review of the remand in custody. Discuss that with your lawyer.' As he spoke he was signing the warrant. Then he glanced briefly at Reimers and Leinen. 'Any further applications?' he asked.

Reimers shook his head and put his files together.

'Yes, I apply for permission to see the files,' said Leinen.

'Noted for the record. Anything else?'

'I apply for a review of the remand in custody in an oral hearing.'

'Also noted.'

'And I apply to be assigned to the accused as court-appointed defence counsel.'

'Here and now? Very well. Any objection from the public prosecutor's office?' asked Köhler.

'No,' said Reimers.

'Then here is my ruling: Caspar Leinen, qualified lawyer, is assigned to the accused, Fabrizio Collini, as court-appointed defence counsel in these proceedings. Is that all?'

Leinen nodded. The secretary took a sheet of paper out of the printer and handed it to Köhler. He looked through it quickly and handed it to Leinen. 'The minutes of this meeting. I'd like your client to sign it, please.'

Leinen stood up, read it and put it down on the wooden board screwed to the grating in front of the defendants' bench to provide a surface for writing on. The ballpoint pen was attached to the wooden board with a thin string. Collini tore it right off, stammered an apology and signed the sheet of paper. Leinen handed it back to the magistrate.

'Well, that's all for today. Officer, please take Herr Collini over to the remand cells. Goodbye, gentlemen,' said the magistrate. The police officer put the handcuffs on Collini's wrists again and left the magistrate's room with him. Leinen and Reimers rose to their feet.

'Oh, Herr Leinen,' said Köhler. 'Wait a moment, would you?'

Leinen turned in the doorway. Reimers left the room.

'I didn't want to ask this in front of your client, but how long have you been qualified?'

'Just over a month.'

'This is the first time you've been present when a warrant for remand in custody was issued?'

'Yes.'

'Then I'll overlook it. But be kind enough to look round this room. Do you see anyone listening to us anywhere?'

'No.'

'Quite correct. There is no one here listening to us, there never was and there never will be. Warrants for remand in custody are not issued in public, nor are requests for reviews of a remand made in public. You do know that, don't you?'

'Yes . . .'

'So why on earth, may I ask, are you wearing a robe in my examination room?'

For a second the examining magistrate seemed to be enjoying Leinen's discomfiture. 'All right, you'll know another time. Good luck with the defence.' He picked up the next file from the stack in front of him.

'Goodbye,' murmured Leinen, but the magistrate did not answer.

Reimers was standing outside the door, waiting

for him. 'You can collect the file from my office on Tuesday, Herr Leinen.'

'Thank you.'

'Didn't you do work experience in our chambers between your examinations?'

'Yes, two years ago. I've only just qualified to practise.'

'I remember,' said Reimers. 'And here's your first murder case already. Well, congratulations. Prospects for the defence aren't good, I'm afraid . . . but we all have to start somewhere.'

Reimers said goodbye and disappeared into a side wing of the building. Leinen slowly went along the corridor towards the exit. He was glad to be alone at last. He looked at the ornamentation above the doors, stucco reliefs. A white pelican pecking her own breast to feed her young with her blood. He sat down on a bench, read the warrant once more, lit a cigarette and stretched his legs.

He'd always wanted to be a defence lawyer. During his work experience, he had been assigned to one of the large sets of chambers that specialized in commercial law. In the weeks after his exams, he received four invitations to go back there for interviews, but he didn't go to any of them. Leinen didn't like those large outfits where up to eight hundred lawyers might be employed. The young men there looked like bankers, had first-class degrees and had bought cars that they couldn't afford; whoever could charge clients for the largest number of hours at the end of the week was the winner. The partners in such large practices already had two marriages under their belts; they wore yellow cashmere sweaters and checked trousers at weekends. Their world consisted of figures, posts on directorial boards, a consultancy contract with the Federal government and a never-ending succession of conference rooms, airport lounges and hotel lobbies. For all of them, it was a disaster if a case came to court: judges were too unpredictable. But that was exactly what Caspar Leinen wanted: to put on a robe and defend his clients. And now here he was.

CHAPTER 3

Caspar Leinen spent the rest of that Sunday beside a lake in Brandenburg, where he had rented a little house for the summer. He passed the time lying on the landing stage, dozing, watching the yachts and the windsurfers. On the way back he looked in at his chambers again, and now he was listening to the message on his answerphone for the tenth time.

'Hello, Caspar, this is Johanna. Please call me back right away.' Then she gave her number, and that was all. He sat down on the floor beside the phone among the boxes, kept pressing the Repeat Message key, leaned his head back against the wall and closed his eyes. It was stuffy in the little room; the air over the city had been stagnant for days.

Johanna's voice hadn't changed. It was still soft, the words still a little too slowly spoken, and suddenly it all came back to him: Rossthal, the green grass under the chestnut trees, the smell of summer when he was a boy.

They lay on the flat roof of the nursery-garden shed, looking up at the sky. The roofing felt was

14

warm underneath them; they had put their jackets under their heads. Philipp told him he'd kissed Ulrike, the baker's daughter.

'And?' asked Caspar. 'Did she let you go any further?'

'Hmm,' said Philipp, leaving it an open question.

The Thermos flask of cold tea stood between them in its faded rattan cover. Philipp's grandfather had brought it back from Africa. They heard the cook calling to them from the terrace of the house, but they stayed put. Here, in the shade of the old trees that Philipp's great-grandfather had planted, everything moved at a leisurely pace on that late-summer afternoon. If things go on like this I'll never get to kiss a girl, thought Caspar. He was twelve; Philipp and he went to the same boarding school on Lake Constance.

Caspar was glad he didn't have to go home in the holidays. His father had inherited some land in Bavaria, part of a forest. He lived alone in a dark forester's house dating from the seventeenth century. The walls were thick, the windows tiny, and there was no central heating. Antlers and stuffed birds hung everywhere. All through his childhood, Caspar had been freezing cold in that house. Both it and his father smelled of soft liquorice in summer – the smell of Ballistol, the oil used for cleaning hunting guns. Ballistol was also used to treat all manner of ailments: it was rubbed on cuts and aching teeth, and even when Caspar had a cough he was given a glass of hot water with some of the oil in it. The only magazine to be found in the house was all about hunting and shooting. The marriage of Caspar's parents had been a mistake. Four years after the wedding, his mother had petitioned for divorce. His father said, later, it was really just because she couldn't stand the way he always went around in gumboots. His mother met another man, known at home only as 'that upstart' because he wore a watch that had cost more than the annual income from the forest. Caspar's mother moved to Stuttgart with her new husband and they had two more children. Caspar stayed with his father in the forester's house until he went to boarding school. He had been ten at the time.

'OK, I suppose we'd better go in,' said Philipp. 'I'm hungry.'

They climbed down from the roof and went over to the house.

'How about a swim afterwards?' asked Philipp.

'I'd rather go fishing,' said Caspar.

'Right, fishing's a better idea. We can grill the fish.'

After the cook had scolded them, and the boys had told her they'd been too far off to hear her calling, there were buttered rolls with ham. As usual, they ate in the kitchen, not upstairs with Philipp's parents. Caspar liked it down there, where countless white kitchen drawers had writing in black ink on them: SALT, SUGAR, COFFEE,

FLOUR, CARAWAY. When the postman came in the morning he sat at the table with the boys and they all looked through the senders' addresses on the letters and read the postcards before they were taken up to Philipp's parents.

Every other afternoon Philipp had extra coaching, and Caspar spent that time with Philipp's grandfather, Hans Meyer, in his office. Sometimes they played chess on a very old board. Meyer was patient with the boy, let him win now and then, and gave him money when he did.

Hans Meyer still ran the family firm. His grandfather had founded the Meyer Works in 1886, and after the Second World War Hans Meyer had built it up into an international concern. The company manufactured all kinds of machinery, as well as surgical instruments, plastic and packaging. At the beginning of the twentieth century Hans Meyer's father had bought a huge tract of marshy land outside the city. He brought in architects and landscape gardeners from Berlin to drain the site and to lay it out as a park, with paved drives, gravel and woodland paths, lawns, exotic trees and an avenue of chestnuts. The stream was dammed to form three pools, and an artificial island stood in the largest; you reached it over a pale blue Chinese bridge. There was a tennis court with a red-sand surface, an open-air swimming pool, a nursery garden, a guesthouse and a house for the chauffeur and his family. Down in the park a path led past lilac bushes to an orangery with glass panes set in lead frames. The main house was built in 1904, on a small rise; a flight of steps outside led up to a stone terrace with four round columns. Although there were over thirty rooms, with six garages accommodated in the side wings, the house had a natural look and seemed to belong in the landscape. The window shutters were always painted dark green, and so it was known in the family simply as the Green House. It was a well-chosen name in other respects too, for ivy grew all over one side of the house, and behind it stood eight old chestnut trees. The family ate supper under their tall crowns on summer weekends.

Hans Meyer was the only person at Rossthal who had time for the children. He told them how to build tree houses without using nails, and where to find the best worms for fishing bait. Once he gave Philipp and Caspar knives with birchwood handles. He showed them how to cut whistles with the knives, and the boys imagined using them to defend the family against any burglars who broke in at night. That was the last summer to be all theirs. The grown-ups didn't bother about them, and they had hardly any concept of time longer than a single day. All that was wrong with their world was that the fish didn't bite and the girls wouldn't kiss.

Four years later Caspar met Johanna, Philipp's sister. He and Philipp were spending all their holidays at Rossthal now. Even at Christmas, it was more fun there than at Caspar's father's cold house. It had begun snowing two weeks before the Christmas celebrations began, and now the snow was so deep that the paths in the park looked like mazes when they were cleared. Philipp and Caspar were sitting in front of the tall fireplace in the entrance hall. The family's three dogs were asleep on the stone floor; they were not allowed in the upper storeys. Philipp was wearing a yellow dressing gown with a plate-sized crest on it; he had found it in a wardrobe in the attic. They were smoking his grandfather's cigars, looking at the fire and planning what to do over the next few days.

Franz, the family's chauffeur, had met Johanna at Munich Airport. She came into the hall through a side door, so Philipp couldn't see her. When Caspar was about to get up she shook her head and put her forefinger to her mouth. Then she crept up behind Philipp's chair and covered his eyes with her hands.

'Who am I?' she asked.

'No idea,' said Philipp. 'No, wait, with those rough hands it's obviously fat Franz!' He laughed, took her hands away from his face and came round the chair to give his sister a hug.

'Hey, that's a handsome dressing gown, Philipp,' she said. 'And such a bright yellow . . .' Then she turned to Caspar. 'You must be Caspar,' she said with composure. He blushed. She leaned forward so that he could kiss her on the cheeks, and he got a glimpse of her white bra. Her face was still cold. Like Philipp, she was tall and slender, but everything that was lanky about him looked elegant in her. She had the same dark eyes and arched eyebrows as her brother, but the mouth in her pale, clear face was soft and humorous. She was only a few years older than Caspar, but she was grown up and unattainable.

She spent the next two days almost constantly on the phone to her friends in England; you could hear her laughter all over the house, and her father was cross because the line was always engaged. When she went back she left a void behind her, although no one but Caspar seemed to notice it.

Next summer Philipp got his first car, a red Citroën 2CV with white seats. It was the last holidays before their final year at school, when they would be taking the school-leaving exam. As usual the two of them worked on the production line in the Meyer Works for the first half of the holidays and spent their earnings in the second half. They took the car over the Brenner Pass to Venice. Philipp's great-grandfather had bought an art nouveau villa on the Lido there in the 1920s. Once they had seen all the museums and churches, the days soon merged into each other: they sailed on the lagoon, played tennis and spent the afternoons in beach cafés, on hotel terraces, or lying in the long, dark green shadows on the quay wall. In the evening they took the water bus to Venice, went to the bars in Cannaregio, and strolled at leisure through the nocturnal streets. They were hardly ever back before early morning, when they would sit on the terrace for another hour, listening to the cry of the seagulls, and all was well with their world.

At the end of the holidays Johanna came from London for a week's visit. On the day of her departure, she was lying beside Caspar after they had been swimming. She propped herself on her elbows, her hair falling over her face. Suddenly she bent over him and looked into his face. He closed his eyes, feeling her wet hair on his forehead; she kissed him on the mouth, and their teeth clashed. 'Don't look so serious,' she said, laughing, and put her hand over his eyes. Then she ran off, back to the sea, turned once again and called, 'Come on, then!' Of course he didn't, but he watched her go, and later he couldn't remember ever being so happy as on those clear blue days beside the sea.

Just under a year later, the boys took their final school exams. After the end-of-year celebrations, Philipp's parents came to drive their son home from the boarding school. On the last bend before you reached the sign saying Rossthal, a low-loader truck laden with timber stood right across the road. It had come out of a field path and had been trying to turn in the narrow lane. The Meyers' car went right under the articulated truck, and the tree trunks it was carrying sliced the car roof off. Philipp's head was torn from his body, and his parents bled to death in the road.

The funeral was held in Rossthal. In church, the priest said what a good son Philipp had been, and what a good grandson, and what a great future he would have had. He didn't mention the fact that the coffin remained closed because the dead body had no head. The priest wore mauve-framed reading glasses; he stood in front of the congregation making the sign of the cross in the air; he spoke of a better world than this. Caspar felt sick. He left the church before Mass was over. Outside, the gravediggers stood in their suits beside the timber struts on which they would place the coffins later. They were smoking and talking, and they were alive. When they saw Caspar they dropped their cigarettes on the earth and ground them out. He didn't want to disturb them, so instead he went to the funerary chapel in the cemetery. He sat down on a marble bench and watched the burial from there in the faint light.

Hans Meyer was burying his son, his daughter-in-law and his grandson. He stood rigid beside the graves, supported by Johanna. He received condolences for four hours on end, saying a few friendly words to everyone. Then he went home and shut himself up in his study. Johanna had herself driven straight to the airport; she didn't want to talk to anyone.

Caspar went to see Hans Meyer in his study that evening. He asked the old man if it would be an idea to play chess as they used to. They played in silence, until after a while Hans Meyer stopped. He opened the window and looked out at the dimly lit park.

'This is something that happened when I was a little boy, maybe eight or nine years old,' said Meyer. He spoke without turning round. 'I had a red-and-blue shirt. Really bright colours; I've no idea what material it was. My uncle had brought it back from Italy. I put my new shirt on and went over to the riding stables. I was there almost every day at the time; I liked the horses a lot. Out in the paddock I saw my mother's showjumper, a nervous animal. It had already won at a number of shows, and my mother thought she stood a good chance of taking it to the Olympic Games in a few years' time. Maybe I just wanted to pat the horse that day – I'd often done that before, but I don't remember now. Anyway, on seeing me the horse reared up and ran into the wooden fencing of the paddock. It took fright, broke its left foreleg and screamed with pain. Horses can scream horribly, and I'd never heard anything like it before. I put my hands over my ears and ran away. That afternoon the forester came and put the poor animal out of its misery.'

Hans Meyer turned. He was shedding silent tears, but his voice was steady. 'That evening I was summoned to my father's study. I sat just where you're sitting now, at that desk. Parents didn't talk to their children much in those days. I loved my father, but I was afraid of him. He said I was to blame for the death of the horse, for causing it to die before its time. And I should take better care of what was entrusted to me in future. "Before its time", those were his words. My father didn't punish me. He said I ought to think about the horse's death . . . A few days later, it was buried in the park by the lower lake. Not the whole horse, of course, only its hooves.'

'I know. Philipp showed me the place once.' Caspar looked at the old man, his friend. 'But it wasn't your fault,' he said.

'What do you mean?'

'Your shirt couldn't have frightened it. Horses don't see colours. They see in black and white, that's all.'

Hans Meyer leaned on the back of the chair; he smiled. 'Well, it's nice of you to say that, Caspar. But it's not true. Horses can see red and blue.'

The old man passed the back of his hand over his eyes. He returned to the window, opened both panes and stood leaning against the frame. Caspar got to his feet and went over to him. Hans Meyer turned round and gave Caspar a hug. Then the old man said he'd like to be alone

24

now. When Caspar drove home next morning, he found the old chess set on the passenger seat of his car.

After the time lost to his military service, Leinen began studying law in Hamburg. He had changed since Philipp's death: he was quiet these days, things seemed strange to him. He often had a sense of being removed from himself, observing himself from the outside, and moving his body as if by remote control. At such times he thought he might have inherited the dark side of his father's character.

He had been back to Rossthal only once since the funeral, when Johanna invited him to her wedding four years after his friend's death. She was marrying an Englishman twenty years her senior who had been her professor at Trinity College, Cambridge; a kindly man with white eyebrows. Everyone thought him entertaining and charming. When Caspar offered his congratulations outside the church after the wedding ceremony she whispered in his ear, saying how much she missed Philipp, and caressed his cheek. He held her arm tightly, kissed the palm of her hand, and for a brief moment he thought that as a couple they might yet be saved.

And now, six years later, he called her phone number from his tiny office. She picked the phone up at the first ring.

'Hello, Johanna.'

'At last! I've been trying to get in touch ever since yesterday. I didn't have your mobile number. Caspar, why are you doing this?'

He was surprised; she sounded furious. 'What do you mean?'

'Why are you defending that bastard?' She began to cry.

'Johanna, do calm down. I don't understand a word you're saying.'

'It's all over the media. You've taken on the defence of that Italian.'

'But . . . wait . . . wait a moment . . .' Leinen got to his feet; his briefcase was still on the desk. He fished the arrest warrant out from among the other papers. 'Johanna, he shot someone called Jean-Baptiste Meyer, that's what the warrant says.'

'My God, Caspar, "Jean-Baptiste" is only the name in his passport.'

'What are you talking about?'

'You're going to be defence counsel for my grandfather's murderer.'

Hans Meyer's mother had been French. She called her son Jean-Baptiste, after John the Baptist. But like many of his generation, he didn't want a long-winded name. If you were called Friedrich in those days you became Fritz; a Reinhard would change his name to Reiner. And Johannes was shortened to Hans. He was known to everyone as plain Hans Meyer; the name was printed that way even on his business cards.

Leinen pictured the dead man for the first time: Hans Meyer, shot in a hotel room, a puddle of blood, police officers, red-and-white barrier tape. He sat down on the floor with his back to the wall. His father's desk stood at an angle in the room; a piece of wood had split off one of its legs.

CHAPTER 4

As usual, no one knew who had been talking to the press. Later, the public prosecutor's office assumed that there had been an informant in the ranks of the police; too many details were given. In any case, the biggest tabloid in Berlin made 'Murder in Luxury Hotel' the lead headline on the front page of its Sunday-evening edition. The name of the killer meant nothing to anyone, but the victim was well known. He was one of the richest men in the Federal Republic: Hans Meyer, owner and chairman of the board of Meyer Engineering Works, holder of the Federal Cross of Merit. Editorial teams in the news media tried to find out more, they sifted through archives, read old reports. Journalists speculated on the motive for the crime. Most of them suspected economic sabotage; no one could say anything for certain.

The lawyer Professor Richard Mattinger was sprawled on his sofa in his dressing gown, thinking about his wife. It was almost twenty years since she had found this house on the Wannsee. At that time, eight years before reunification, properties here on the lake had been ridiculously cheap, and new families had moved into the old houses. His wife had been right: the value of real estate had greatly increased in the last ten years. She died soon after she had furnished the house, and Mattinger had refused to change anything in it since then.

His dressing gown was open, showing the white hair on his chest. He was letting his girlfriend, a very young Ukrainian woman, masturbate him. She told him how much she loved him countless times every day. Mattinger didn't care. He knew that a relationship like theirs was always a reciprocal business deal – at best agreeable to both parties for a while. He was in his mid-sixties, still fit and active. In the last days of the war, when he was eight years old, a hand grenade had torn off his left forearm. But his eyes were his most striking feature, dark blue and of enormous intensity.

The telephone rang for the ninth time. Only a few people had his private number, and it must be important if someone was calling him on a Sunday afternoon. When he finally picked up the phone, his girlfriend looked up from between his knees, smiled, and asked if she should go on. It took Mattinger a moment to concentrate his mind. He jammed the receiver between his shoulder and his head, slid a notepad across the coffee table towards him and began taking notes. When he had hung up again, he got to his feet, closed his dressing gown, caressed the girl's head and went into his study without a word.

Half an hour later, he had his driver take him to his chambers. On the way, he called one of the young lawyers he employed and asked him to come to the office. Mattinger had acted for the defence in the terrorist trials of the 1970s in Stammheim Prison; his appearances in court had been media events. A weekly magazine had once written of him that he had a mind of 'almost dazzling intelligence'. In those days, perhaps for the first time in German legal history, the rights of the defendants had to be genuinely fought for. At the beginning of the student riots many thought democracy itself was endangered, and terrorists were regarded first and foremost as enemies of the state. Even before the verdict was given, a prison had been built for the defendants. Laws were changed on account of these trials, defence lawyers shouted at the judges, defendants went on hunger strike, and the presiding judge had to stand down from the main trial for reasons of bias. War was waged in court. The defending lawyers learned something new; they became more self-confident, and understood, better than ever before, that justice can be done only in a fair trial. It was too much for many of them. They made common cause with their clients, overstepped the boundary, and became offenders themselves. Tragedies born of rage. Mattinger was different. The public thought he had lent the terrorists his voice, which was clearer and more effective than their own. But that was not so. Of course he had been to demonstrations a few times, had met the students' spokesmen, but it had alarmed him to see how their own words intoxicated them. In point of fact, Mattinger represented only legality. He was a believer in the constitutional state founded on law.

Since then he had acted as defence counsel in almost two thousand trials. He had never yet lost in a murder trial; none of his clients had received a life sentence. But as time went on his clientele changed. First came the speculators and building contractors, then the bankers, the company chairmen, the old-established families. It was a long time since he'd defended a drug dealer, an underworld boss or a murderer. These days he wrote articles in legal journals, he was chairman of a number of legal associations and a visiting professor at the Humboldt University in Berlin. He lived in an altogether more prestigious world now. He seldom appeared in court; most proceedings against his clients were dropped by the state prosecutor's office in return for large payments, without ever coming to a full-scale trial. Mattinger still believed in the constitutional state founded on law, but the battles seemed already to have been won. Sometimes, when he was stuck waiting at an airport overnight, he felt as though he had mislaid something. But he didn't want to stop and work out exactly what.

By the time he reached his chambers, he had already phoned the murder squad. Of course, he knew the top police officers there, and they came up with enough information for him to form a vague idea of events. Two hours later he had the Meyer Works company lawyer, Holger Baumann, on the phone. Mattinger and the young lawyer from his chambers were sitting in one of the large conference rooms, talking to Baumann on speakerphone. The company lawyer told them that the firm employed over forty thousand people worldwide, with profits year on year almost 4 per cent above the industry average, and they were on the brink of bringing off the biggest deal in their entire history. The murder of Hans Meyer, former chairman of the board and main shareholder of the company, was a catastrophe, said Baumann. They didn't want the firm all over the papers. He mentioned the bribery case involving a subsidiary a few years ago, and the trial in which Mattinger had represented a leading employee who worked there. There had been unwelcome publicity in the papers at the time. Baumann sounded nervous. Mattinger remembered that he had never liked the man.

No one in the firm, Baumann continued, had any idea why Meyer had been murdered. The old man had still been chairman, but he was sure it was nothing to do with the firm. Mattinger was surprised. The crime was only a few hours old, and Baumann could already say he was sure of that.

The board, he went on, wanted Mattinger to represent the firm in the murder trial. Mattinger explained that that wasn't possible: only a family member could ask him to act as accessory prosecutor. Most civil lawyers, he added, weren't aware of it, but that was the law. Baumann promised to see about that, and another hour later there was a fax on Mattinger's desk from the murder victim's granddaughter and sole heir, Johanna Meyer, sent from London.

Mattinger promised Johanna Meyer that he would take care of everything. Tomorrow he would speak to the public prosecution office in Berlin and then report back to all concerned. His young colleague went into his office and did the paperwork.

At around eleven o'clock Mattinger was home again. His girlfriend was already asleep, in the guestroom as usual. He got himself a glass of iced water from the kitchen and went into the garden. There was a smell of freshly mown grass. He took off his tie and unbuttoned his shirt. It was still too hot. He pressed the cold glass to his forehead. The extraordinary meeting of the board

33

in Munich had been fixed for three o'clock the following afternoon. Mattinger wouldn't have any answers by then. He didn't even know the right questions.

CHAPTER 5

Leinen spent the first night after Collini's arrest writing a petition. He sat at the kitchen table in his apartment with legal textbooks and commentaries open in front of him. There was a small black-and-white TV set on the table as well. Most of the time he kept it turned on with the sound muted. However, when the news headlines came on at ten-thirty there was a short film about the dead man, pictures with a few brief comments: Hans Meyer with Konrad Adenauer, Hans Meyer with Ludwig Erhard, Hans Meyer with Helmut Kohl. The presenter said the motive for the murder was not clear, and the public prosecutor's office was still investigating. More pictures showed the Hotel Adlon, the remand prison, the police station where the murder squad was based. The alleged murderer, said the presenter, was an Italian citizen.

At around five in the morning Leinen printed out the petition he had drafted; at seven he had the final version. The text had turned out well, but he wasn't sure that it would do him much good. He was petitioning to step down from Collini's defence, asking the examining magistrate to rescind his duty to provide legal aid in this case.

At seven-thirty he left his apartment. It had been raining, and the air was cool and fresh now. He went to a news kiosk and bought all the daily papers. The murder of Meyer was on nearly every front page.

On the ground floor of Leinen's building, two storeys below his apartment, there was a bakery, or rather a 'bake shop', an Identikit branch of a large chain. The baker was a very fat man, red-faced, with small hands: his knuckles looked like dimples on the backs of them. He could move surprisingly fast, but he was too stout for the narrow space behind the display shelves, and the counter cut into his big belly, leaving a line of breadcrumbs on his apron. The baker had put three old wooden chairs outside his shop, and in summer Leinen would sit there on the pavement every morning, drinking coffee and eating one of the poor-quality croissants. Sometimes the baker joined him. Today he said Leinen was looking terrible.

Leinen took the suburban train to the courthouse building. A busker with a guitar went along the carriages bawling out a Bob Dylan song; no one but a few tourists gave him any money. Just after eight Leinen was at the Moabit Criminal Court building.

The Capital Crimes Department of the public prosecutor's office was on the third floor, with steel-framed armoured glass in the windows looking out on the corridor. He had done three months' work experience in this department, and knew most of the public prosecutors here, at least by sight. The court registry office was stacked high with files up to the ceiling, in pigeonholes, on shelves, desks and the floor, arranged according to some unfathomable principle. All the paperwork to do with cases of violent death ended up here. There were files on all kinds of killings: murder, manslaughter, suicide bombings, hostage-taking ending in death. Postcards sent by secretaries when they were away on holiday were pinned up on the walls: sunsets, beaches, palm trees. Computer monitors bristled with photos of children and husbands.

Leinen gave the reference number of the file and showed the clerk in the registry the document naming him as court-appointed defence counsel. She gave him a thin folder. She too knew Leinen from his work experience here, and wished him luck with the case. It would be difficult for the defence, she said, looking at him sympathetically. Richard Mattinger had already said he would be appearing as counsel in the accessory prosecution. Leinen also learned that the autopsy on the body was to be at one o'clock in the Forensic Institute.

He took the file and wondered whether he ought to visit his client, but he couldn't think of anything that he could usefully discuss with Collini. He leafed through the pages while he walked down the corridors to the lawyers' room.

The defending lawyers' common room in the Moabit Criminal Court was a safe haven; no client, no judge, not even the interpreters were allowed in. It had existed since the days of the Weimar Republic, and famous defence lawyers such as Max Alsberg had frequented it in the 1920s. It hadn't changed much to this day. The lawyers read the newspapers there, phoned the registry offices, wrote their pleas or waited for a trial to resume. You could hire a robe for a euro; the secretary took a note of phone calls, and sometimes offered sweets to lawyers she liked. But above all this was where defence counsel chatted. They exchanged gossip about judges and public prosecutors, discussed trials, shared advice on petitions, made and dissolved alliances. If a judge did not stick to an agreement, or a public prosecutor withheld information, this was where defence counsel heard about it. They talked frankly, admitted to failures and boasted of success. In here they spoke of their clients in different terms, and cracked jokes about the crimes to help them cope with the stress. The coffee came from a vending machine and tasted of plastic and powdered milk. The furnishings were rather shabby, the upholstery of the sofas threadbare.

Leinen headed for the copiers at the back of the room, and was still reading the file as he crossed the lawyers' room. He collided with another lawyer, papers fell to the floor. Leinen apologized, picked the papers up and went on. When he was standing by the copier he saw Richard Mattinger on a sofa reading the newspapers. Leinen went over to him.

'Good morning, Herr Mattinger,' he said. 'I'm Caspar Leinen. We're appearing in the same trial.'

'Fabrizio Collini? The Hans Meyer case?'

'Yes, that's right.'

Mattinger stood up and shook hands. 'May I offer you a cup of coffee?' he said.

'Thanks, yes. It's good to meet you,' said Leinen. 'I went to a lecture you gave on criminal proceedings.'

'I trust I didn't talk too much nonsense,' said Mattinger, going over to the coffee maker with Leinen. He put a coin in the slot. The two lawyers waited for the machine to disgorge a brown plastic beaker. 'I hope no one's had tomato soup yet this morning, or the next fifty cups of coffee will taste appalling.'

'Thank you. It's pretty bad to start with.' They went back to the sofa and sat down.

'Well, congratulations, Herr Leinen, this is going to be a great case,' said Mattinger.

'Anything but, I'm afraid,' murmured Leinen.

'Why do you say that?'

'I'm actually trying to back out of defending the client. I stupidly put myself down on the roster of court-appointed defence counsel, but I can't go on with the defence in this case. You'll read about it in the file anyway, so I might as well tell you now.' And Leinen explained what had happened. Mattinger asked if he could read his petition to withdraw from the case, and Leinen handed him a copy.

'Yes, you put it very well,' said Mattinger a few minutes later. 'And what you say is perfectly understandable. I'm just not sure if it's enough. You know that legally you can be relieved of the duty to give legal aid only if a relationship of trust between you and your client has fallen through. And Judge Köhler is a stickler for the letter of the law. I'd almost call him a technocrat.'

'I'm going to try anyway,' said Leinen.

'We don't know each other, Herr Leinen, and you won't welcome advice from me.'

'No, really,' said Leinen. 'I'd like to know what you think.'

'I'm assuming this is your first big murder case?'

'Yes,' said Leinen, nodding.

'In your place, I wouldn't put in that petition.'

Leinen looked at him in astonishment. 'But . . . I practically grew up in the Meyer family.'

Mattinger shook his head. 'So? In the next trial,

the murder may remind you of some tragic child-hood experience of your own. And the case after that could keep reminding you of a girlfriend you once had who was raped. Then again, you might not like your client's nose, or you'll think the drugs he deals in are the worst evils to afflict mankind. You want to be a defence lawyer, Herr Leinen, so you must act like one. You've under-taken to defend a man. Right, maybe that was a mistake, but it was your mistake, not his. Now you're responsible for the man, you're all he has. You should tell him about your relationship with the victim, and then ask if he still wants you to defend him. If he does – and this is the only crucial point – you must do your best for him, make an effort, present your case to the best of your ability. This is a murder trial, not a university seminar.'

Leinen wasn't sure whether Mattinger was right, or whether he just wanted to be facing an inexperienced adversary in the trial. The old lawyer was looking at him with a friendly expression. Maybe it was both.

'I'll think it over,' said Leinen at last. 'Many thanks anyway.'

'I must be off too,' said Mattinger. 'I have to see someone in the commercial law department. But I wonder, would you like to drop in at my chambers this afternoon? Maybe it would make sense for us to discuss a few things.'

'I'd like that.' Leinen realized that Mattinger would want to find out how, if he stayed with his brief, he was planning to defend Collini. But he very much wanted to know the great lawyer better.

CHAPTER 6

Watching an autopsy for the first time, you encounter your own death. Modern man isn't used to the sight of dead bodies; they have disappeared entirely from the everyday world. Sometimes you see a fox lying dead at the roadside, knocked down by a car, but most of us have never set eyes on a human corpse.

When Leinen entered the Forensic Institute, Dr Reimers, the senior public prosecutor, and two police officers from the murder squad were already waiting for the head of Forensic Medicine, Professor Wagenstett. It was unusual for a defending lawyer to attend an autopsy, but Leinen wanted to know everything about the case.

The autopsy table was 2.5 metres long and 85 centimetres wide. It rested on a broad central pedestal, with two power points in the side for the electric saws and drills, a water tap that you could turn on and off with your knee, and a shower handset. The sink was set into the table. It was a modern model with a surface that could be electrically raised or lowered. 'Almost silent,' Wagenstett had said when the table was delivered six months earlier, happy as a boy with a new toy. Below the perforated surface – which was in three parts to allow easy cleaning – a receptacle carried blood and other residues down a slight slope to a removable filter. The fume extractor above the table looked like an outsize kitchen-cooker hood.

When Leinen saw the body he felt sick. The dead man was naked. Under the harsh white light, the hair on his chest and around his genitals looked thick, his nipples and fingernails were dark, every contrast was emphasized. Half the dead man's face was torn away, with muscle fibre and bone exposed. The remaining eye was open, torn and milky. Like the eye of a fish, thought Leinen.

Wagenstett began the autopsy. Using his thumbs, he pressed the livor mortis marks on the torso and legs. His assistant, a sturdy female medical student with her hair pinned up, bent over the body with him.

'The marks are dark purple,' Wagenstett pronounced. 'The body was not lying out of doors. That agrees with the police report.' He turned to his assistant. 'Look, the marks give way only slightly under strong pressure; they won't go back to their previous state within the next few seconds. Try it for yourself.'

She tried it.

'What do you conclude from that?' asked Wagenstett.

'The man has been dead more than six hours and less than thirty-six hours.'

'Correct.' Wagenstett straightened up. He was very much the teacher again. 'Define those marks, will you?'

'Livor mortis marks show when the force of gravity causes blood to settle inside the vessels.'

'Yes, that's right. Good.'

It went on like this for about two hours. Wagenstett dictated into a small microphone hanging above the table. Rigor mortis of the muscles had set in almost entirely. No putrefaction yet. Wagenstett picked up the report by the doctor who had attended the scene of the crime, read the data he gave on body temperature and the temperature outside the body, and nodded. Then he described the dead man: head, hair (length, height of hairline above the forehead), face, nasal structure and nostrils ('shattered, blood and clear fluid drained away, tracks running to both ears, conspicuous on the right'), the eyes ('left eye destroyed, not present, right eye partially present, conjunctiva pale'), the mouth cavity ('containing reddish fluid'). Wagenstett spoke quietly and with concentration. The outward appearance of the corpse, he told his assistant, was their first contact with the dead man. One must proceed carefully, slowly and respectfully. Examine the body from top to bottom, systematically, not jumping back and forth between striking features. 'The man is dead,' said Wagenstett, 'so take your time.' He treated the body with dignity; jokes were banned at the autopsy table.

After the outer appearance of the corpse came

the internal examination. Leinen had to lean against the tiled wall; his legs felt weak. Wagenstett had turned the heavy body over and was dissecting the back. With a scalpel, he cut down from the nape of the neck to the sacrum and then over both buttocks, so that his incision was Y-shaped. He separated the tissues layer by layer, removing the muscles of the back, turning the soft tissue and the left shoulder blade to one side. Leinen closed his eyes, but the smell was still there. He wanted to leave, but he was unable to move.

Between the top layers of the scalp and the bone lies a membrane suffused with blood vessels and easily removed from the pericranium. Scalping does not take much force. Wagenstett taught his students that the family of the dead have a right to a corpse looking as intact as possible. For that reason, they should make an incision at the back of the head and move the scalp towards the forehead until the skull is exposed. Then it could simply be sawn apart and the brain removed. After that you pulled the scalp down again and stitched it up so that the corpse still had a head.

'However, in this case that won't do,' Wagenstett explained. 'We must make the incision elsewhere; we need to find the path of the bullets.' Latin terms followed, Wagenstett dictated, made an incision from ear to ear, and removed the still-intact scalp. A projectile fell from the jelly-like matter in the exposed wound to the metal table. Two more had lodged in the top of the skull, and a fourth had made its exit through the left eye socket. Wagenstett showed the lumps of metal to Reimers, the senior public prosecutor. 'Greatly distorted. Ballistics will have a tough time with these,' the professor said.

Then came the long, thin probes to be used in reconstructing the course taken by the bullets. Wagenstett inserted them in the 'breaks in the skin', as he described the entry wounds. They stuck a few centimetres out of the skull. Leinen thought they made the head look like a baroque icon: a saint's head with rays of light shining from a halo. Wagenstett took photographs, and for some time there was no sound except for the flash charging.

The autopsy went on for another hour; every wound, every haemorrhage, every splintered bone was measured and recorded. There were old scars: on both knees (5 and 8 centimetres), on the right elbow (2 centimetres), a 6-centimetre scar on the belly from an operation to remove the appendix, a 7-millimetre scar above the left elbow, a 9-millimetre scar on the chin. The organs were removed, examined and weighed (brain 1380 g, heart 340 g, right lung 790 g, left lung 630 g, spleen 150 g, liver 1060 g, right kidney 175 g, left kidney 180 g). Blood from the thighs and the heart, urine, stomach contents, liver and lung tissue, and liquid from the gall bladder were assessed. The kicks were described as precisely as possible, and the marks left by the heel of the killer's shoe were photographed. Wagenstett dictated the findings of

47

the autopsy and the conclusions to be drawn from them. Dr Reimers stood up to stretch his legs. He would get the report next day, he was told, they were overworked in the secretaries' office. Then Professor Wagenstett stitched the body up again.

The two murder squad officers were the first to leave the autopsy room. Leinen, unable to speak, did not say goodbye to anyone. One of the two police officers was wearing a blue-and-white-striped shirt. Leinen stared at the shirt and began counting the stripes. He saw nothing but the shirt, concentrating on the stripes until he was outside. Then he stood on the flight of steps leading up to the brick building of the Forensic Institute, where he felt the full force of the midday heat. He reached for the silver cigarette case in his jacket pocket. It was cold, and it was real. Hands shaking, he lit a cigarette. Reimers came out to stand beside him, saying something. Leinen couldn't take it in until he was past the first couple of comments:

'. . . the case seems cut and dried. All the shots fired from behind and above. Presumably the first when he was on his knees, the others when he was down on the floor. No sign of any attempt at self-defence, the victim can't have suspected anything. I'm sorry, Herr Leinen, but it all points to a charge of murder.' Reimers had taken off his jacket and rolled up his sleeves. There were dark marks on his shirt collar. 'My God, it's hot,' he said.

'Yes,' said Leinen. His mouth was dry, his tongue furred.

'Have a word with your client; maybe he'll say why he did it after all. That's usually the best course to take in a situation like this.'

'I'll do that. Thanks.'

Leinen went to his car, only to find it boxed in by a delivery van. He sat down in the shade on the warm slate slabs of a gateway entrance. It was quiet here. The pollen of a chestnut tree had dusted the pavement and the strip of grass red; light was refracted on the hot tarmac, making the street mirror the sky like a stretch of water. I can simply take the plate off my office door again and forget all about this, thought Leinen.

CHAPTER 7

At five in the afternoon Leinen rang the doorbell of Mattinger's chambers. Reception for visitors was in the Berlin Room, as it was called, a large room with only one window. It linked the façade to the lateral wings and the back of the building. One of the secretaries told Leinen to go straight through; Herr Mattinger was expecting him. Leinen knocked at his door, waited, heard nothing and went in.

The room was dark, not much larger than Leinen's own office, with a simple desk, a wooden chair with arms at the desk, no visitors' chairs, a yellow lamp, a black phone with a circular dial. The walls were panelled in mahogany, bookshelves were built into the side walls, and there were broad wooden venetian blinds over both windows. It looked like an office from the 1920s. A large cigar box stood on the desk, black wood with pale intarsia work. Mattinger had his feet up on the desk and was dozing; his tie had slipped, saliva trickled from the right-hand corner of his mouth. A few red files lay in front of him; Leinen could see from the names on them that they were being dealt with by other lawyers in the chambers. Mattinger woke with a jolt, saw Leinen, wiped his mouth and stood up. 'How are you, Herr Leinen?' he asked. He didn't reek of alcohol, but the sweetish odour of a man who habitually drinks too much clung to him. 'You look tired.'

'Thanks, you're the third person to say so today.'

'Then it's probably true. Come along, we'll be too cramped in here. Let's sit on the balcony.'

'I like your room.'

'I bought it thirty years ago from a building on the Kurfürstendamm that was being renovated, had it installed here. It's said to have belonged to a famous notary.'

'It's wonderful.'

'Maybe a little too dark,' said Mattinger. 'But I'm used to that by now.'

They went through two large conference rooms to the balcony, where they sat on pale rattan outdoor furniture under an awning. It had been raining; steam rose from the street.

Mattinger went back into one of the conference rooms. Leinen heard him speaking to the secretaries in their office, ordering drinks. When he came back he took a cigar case out of his jacket, a well-worn leather case. In his pinstriped suit, Mattinger himself looked like someone from the 1920s.

'Do you smoke cigars? No? What a pity.' He took a cigar cutter from his waistcoat pocket, twisted it slowly in the end of the cigar and drew out the remains of tobacco with it. Using an extra-long match, he lit the cigar. Although he had to do everything with one hand, he made it look easy. 'I've been making inquiries about you, Leinen.'

'Really?'

'Distinction in both your state examinations, best of your year in criminal law, assistant to the professor of criminology at Humboldt University, fifteen publications in legal journals.' Mattinger drew on his cigar. 'I've read them all. Some of them are really first class.'

'Thank you.'

'You had offers that would have allowed you to stay on at the university or be appointed a judge. You turned both down. You wanted to be a practising lawyer. Your professor considers that you have a brilliant mind, but he also described you as obstinate and pig-headed.' Mattinger laughed.

Leinen laughed with him, but he felt uncomfortable. 'He'd say a thing like that to you?'

'Your professor and I have known each other for a hundred years. I like to know what sort of person I'm dealing with.'

The secretary brought coffee and water. They talked about judges and public prosecutors. Meanwhile Leinen watched Mattinger blowing cigar smoke into the air. Gradually he relaxed.

'Well, what have you decided, Leinen? Are you going to defend Collini?'

'I'm not sure yet. I've just been at the autopsy. It was grisly.'

'Yes, it always is. You don't want to see the corpse as a human being. On the table it's only a subject for scientific study. Once you understand that, the process actually becomes interesting. But one probably never gets over the shock of it entirely.'

Leinen examined Mattinger. His skin was brown, deep lines ran horizontally and vertically across his forehead, there were crow's feet at the corners of his bright eyes. Leinen had read somewhere that in spite of his disability, Mattinger had sailed solo from Hamburg to South America a few years ago.

'Once again, if you do defend him, how do you estimate your chances?'

'Poor. Bloodstains on his clothing, powder marks left on his hands, his fingerprints on the gun and the cartridge cases, on the desk and the bedstead in the hotel. He called the police himself and sat in the hotel lobby waiting to be arrested. There's no other potential murderer in the frame. So . . . it probably won't be a defence expecting an acquittal.'

'Maybe you can get the charge reduced from murder to manslaughter.'

'As I understand it, Hans Meyer was shot from behind. That suggests murder. But I don't know enough yet. It depends what Collini says. And whether he'll testify in court at all.'

'How about the motive? The newspapers are saying that nothing is known about the motive.' Mattinger suddenly turned to Leinen and looked directly at him.

Those eyes of his are hypnotic, thought Leinen. 'That's right, and I don't know anything either. Hans Meyer was a thoroughly decent man. I have no idea why anyone would want to shoot him.'

'A decent man, eh?' Mattinger turned away again. 'They're few and far between. I'm sixty-four and I've known only two thoroughly decent men in my entire life. One of them has been dead for ten years and the other is a monk in a French monastery. Believe me, Leinen, people aren't black or white . . . they're grey.'

'Sounds like a stock phrase,' said Leinen.

Mattinger laughed. 'The older you get, the more you find that clichés are sometimes right.'

The two men drank coffee, each pursuing his own thoughts.

'It's too late for it today,' said Mattinger after a while, 'but you should go to see your client tomorrow and ask him if he wants you to defend him.'

Leinen knew that the old lawyer was right. His client had been in prison for days and he hadn't even asked him yet why he had killed Hans Meyer. Then he realized that he was almost dropping off to sleep. 'Excuse me,' he said. 'I must go home. I was working all last night and I'm really tired now.'

Mattinger rose to his feet and accompanied Leinen to the door. Leinen went down the broad staircase of the building, which dated from the 1870s: red sisal carpet on the stairs, green marble walls. On the last landing he turned to look back once; he hadn't heard the door of the chambers close. Mattinger was still standing up there in the doorway, watching him.

CHAPTER 8

The Royal Remand Prison had been built in 1877 and repeatedly modernized since. It was a red-brick building, with three floors arranged in a star shape around a circular central hall. These days it was known as Moabit Remand Prison. Offenders remanded in custody had been accommodated here for over a hundred and twenty years; the cells were only a few square metres large, each containing a bed, a table, a chair, a cupboard, a washbasin and a toilet. Fabrizio Collini was Prisoner No. 284/01-2, Section II, Cell 145. The woman officer behind the glass pane looked for the name on her list. Leinen showed her the document with the district court's decision, and she entered his name on another list. Collini could now receive post from him uncensored by a magistrate. She called a prison officer and asked him to bring Collini in to see the lawyer.

Leinen waited outside one of the small interview rooms used by lawyers. Police officers escorting inmates passed him. They discussed the prisoners as if they were inanimate objects: 'Where are you taking yours? Mine's on his way back from the doctor . . .' It wasn't that the officers despised the prisoners; most of them didn't even want to know what offences they were charged with. They just spoke, as they always had, a simple language.

Fabrizio Collini came down the corridor. Once again, Leinen was intrigued by his size; he couldn't even see the officer following Collini. They went into the interview room. It was painted with yellow gloss to two-thirds of the way up the walls; it contained a Formica table, two chairs and a washbasin. There was a small window high up on the front wall of the room, an empty biscuit tin did duty as an ashtray, a red alarm bell was fitted beside the door. The place smelled of cigarettes, food and sweat. Leinen sat down with his back to the window, Collini sat opposite him. He was wearing the blue prison uniform; the murder squad had taken his own clothes away.

Leinen told his client about his friendship with the Meyers, and watched Collini's heavy, bony face. Collini did not react.

'We have to clear this point up, Herr Collini. Is my friendship with the Meyers a problem for you?'

'No,' said Collini. 'He's dead. I'm not interested in it any more.'

'Not interested in what?'

'Meyer and his family.'

'But you're probably going to be charged with murder. You could get a life sentence.'

Collini placed both hands on the table. 'Well, I did it.'

Leinen stared at the huge man's mouth. It was true, Collini had done it. The man had shot Meyer in the head four times; it was his fault that the forensic pathologists had cut up Caspar's friend and turned him into a legal case. The man had kicked Hans Meyer's face until the heel came off his shoe. Leinen remembered that face: the lines on it, the thin lips, Meyer's laughter. The law expects too much of me, thought Leinen, I can't defend this man, I can hardly bear to look at him. 'But why did you kill him?' asked Leinen, pulling himself together.

Collini was examining his hands. 'I did it with these hands,' he said.

'Yes, you did it. But why? You must tell me why.'

'I don't want to talk about it.'

'I can't defend you by telling the court that.'

The shadow of the steel grating in front of the high window stood out indistinctly on the yellow wall. From the corridor, he heard the woman officer calling prisoners' names out in the corridor. Collini took a packet of cigarettes out of his breast pocket, tapped a cigarette out of it and put it in his mouth. 'Do you have a light?' he asked.

Leinen shook his head.

Collini got to his feet and went over to the washbasin, then to the door, then back to the washbasin again. Leinen realized that Collini was searching for a lighter, and suddenly he was sorry he didn't have one on him.

'Would you be prepared to make a confession? If we lose on the murder charge, that would still give the court grounds to reduce your sentence. Would you do that?'

Collini sat down again. His eyes seemed to be fixed on a certain point on the bare wall.

'Would you at least do that? You only have to say how you killed him. Not why, only how. Do you understand me?'

After a long pause, Collini said, 'Yes.' Simply, 'Yes,' that was all. He rose to his feet. 'I'd rather go back to the cell now.'

Leinen nodded. Collini went to the door. They didn't shake hands. Their conversation had lasted less than fifteen minutes.

The police officer on duty was waiting outside for him, a stout man with a fat neck, his light brown uniform shirt stretched taut over his paunch and showing his vest between the lower buttons. He looked at Collini's chest and spoke as if to empty air. 'Right, off we go.'

Collini and the officer walked away, side by side, but before they reached the first barred door something odd happened. Collini simply stopped in the middle of the corridor and seemed to be thinking. 'What is it now?' asked the officer. Collini did not reply, only stood there motionless, looking down at the toecaps of his shoes for almost a minute. Then he took a deep breath, turned, and went back to the visitors' room that Leinen had used. The prison officer shrugged his shoulders and followed him. Without knocking, Collini opened the door. 'Herr Leinen,' he said. Leinen was just putting his things together, and looked up at him in surprise. 'Herr Leinen, I know it isn't easy for you. I'm sorry. Just wanted to say thank you.' Collini nodded to Leinen. He did not seem to be expecting an answer, but turned round and went back down the corridor, walking with his legs wide apart, not in any hurry.

Trying to find his way back to the lawyers' exit, Leinen went in the wrong direction, until a woman officer stopped him and told him which way to go. Then he had to wait for a few minutes outside the bulletproof-glass door for the opening system to operate. The plaster above the door was flaking off. He looked at the police officers checking ID and entering names in notebooks. Here, where the remand prisoners were in their cells, waiting to be found guilty or acquitted, he was in a small, narrow world. No professors here, no textbooks, no discussions. All of it was serious and final. He could try to get rid of his legal aid defence brief. He didn't have to defend Collini; the man had killed his friend. It would be easy to end it by saying no; anyone would understand that.

Outside, he took a taxi and went home. The fat baker was sitting on one of the wooden chairs outside his shop, under a sun umbrella.

'How are you?' asked Leinen.

'Hot,' said the baker. 'But it's even hotter inside.'

Leinen sat down, tipped his chair back against the wall and squinted at the sun. He thought of Collini.

'And how are *you*?' asked the baker.

'I just don't know what to do.'

'What's the problem?'

'I don't know whether I ought to defend a man or not. He killed another man, someone I knew well.'

'But you're a lawyer.'

'Hmm . . .' Leinen nodded.

'You know something? I roll the shutter up at five every morning, put the light on and wait for the chilled truck to arrive from the factory. I push the prepared dough into the convection ovens, and then all day, from seven onward, I'm selling the stuff that was delivered. When the weather's bad I sit inside, when it's fine I sit here in the sun. I'd rather make real bread in a real bakery, with real equipment and real ingredients. But it just isn't that way.'

A woman with a Dalmatian passed them and went into the shop. The baker stood up and followed her. A few moments later he came back, bringing two glasses of iced water.

'See what I mean?' asked the baker.

'Not entirely.'

'Maybe I'll have a proper bakery again some day. I did have one, but I lost it in the divorce. Now I work here, that's all there is to it. Simple.' He emptied his glass of water in a single draught and crunched an ice cube. 'You're a lawyer, you have to do what lawyers do.'

They sat in the shade and watched the passers-by. Leinen thought of his father. In his world, everything seemed clear and simple, there were no secrets. His father had not wanted him to become a defence lawyer. It was no profession for a decent man, he had said, everything legal was too complicated for that. Leinen remembered a duck shoot one winter. His father had fired his gun, and a mallard crashed down on the ice of the pond. The dog his father had at the time was still young, and had run off to retrieve the duck without waiting for his master's signal. The ice in the middle of the pond was thin, the dog broke through it, but he wasn't giving up. He swam through the ice-cold water and brought the duck to land. Without a word, his father took off his jacket and rubbed the dog dry with the lining. He carried him home in the jacket. For two days, his father sat in front of the fire with the dog on his knees. When the animal was better, he gave him to a family in the village. He'd never make a gun dog, he had said.

Leinen told the baker that he was probably right, and went home to his apartment. That evening he called Johanna. He said he had no option, he'd have to go on with Collini's defence. He had persuaded his client to confess to committing the crime, but that was as much as he could do. It was a long conversation. Johanna was furious at first, then helpless, and finally desperate. She kept on and on asking why that man had done it. She called him only 'that man'. She was crying.

'Shall I come over there to see you?' he asked, when they'd said everything there was to say. She did not reply for a long time. In the silence, he heard her wooden bangles clicking against each other.

'Yes,' she said at last, 'but I need time.'

When they ended the call, he felt tired and lonely.

Two weeks later Fabrizio Collini confessed to the murder. The interrogation room in the old building in Keithstrasse was cramped: two pale grey desks, a window, mugs of luke-warm coffee. Collini's chair was too small for him. Two police officers had prepared the interrogation, the files from the public prosecutor's office lay in front of them, with yellow Post-its on the pages that they wanted to ask about. The older officer was head of this department of the murder squad; he had three grown-up children and a weakness for chocolate. Thirty-six years in the police had made him not cynical, but calm and composed. He saw defendants as human beings, got them to talk and listened to them. The other police officer was still new here. He had come in from the drugs-related crimes department, and he was nervous. He went to the shooting range more often than his colleagues, his shoes were polished to a shine every morning, and he spent his leisure time at the gym.

This younger officer put a folder of pictures in front of Collini: photographs of the scene of the crime on yellow cardboard, over-sharp shots of the murder victim's shattered head. Leinen was just about to protest when the older officer told his colleague that the pictures weren't necessary; Collini was confessing to the crime anyway. He tried to pick up the folder, but Collini had put his large hands on it and was pressing it down on the desk. When the older officer let go of the folder, Collini pulled it towards him and opened it. Leaning forward, he looked at every single picture. He took his time. No one in the room said a word. When he had finished, he closed the folder and pushed it back over the desk. 'He's dead,' said Collini, looking down at the desk. Then he told them how he had pretended to be a journalist and fixed a date for an interview with Meyer's secretary, and how he had then gone into the hotel suite and killed him. Asked about the murder weapon, he said he had bought it at a flea market in Italy.

Leinen sat beside his client, now and then correcting a phrase that the police officers were about to put on record, but otherwise he drew little stick men on a notepad. He had explained to Collini that a defendant could always keep silent, but if he confessed to the crime the judge had to take it into account and pass a more lenient sentence. That didn't apply to murder, for which the sentence was always life. But in a case of manslaughter the confession was a help.

After two hours the police officers had no more questions to ask about the crime itself. Leinen got to his feet and told them that the interrogation was now over.

'If you don't mind, we were about to come to the heart of the matter – your client's motive, Herr Leinen. We have to talk about the motive,' said the older police officer.

'I'm sorry.' Leinen remained courteous. He put his notepad back in his briefcase. 'Fabrizio Collini has confessed to the crime. He's not going to say any more.'

The police officers protested, but Leinen was not giving way. The older man sighed and put his files together; he realized there was nothing he could do. The younger police officer wasn't giving up. When the bulletproof minibus came to the police station in the late afternoon to take the prisoner back to jail, he got into the back seat with Collini. He could talk even without his lawyer present, he told him. Leinen was certainly a nice lad, but young and without any experience of murder cases. Young lawyers often failed to give their clients the right advice, he said, they just made matters worse.

Collini didn't even look at him; he seemed to be asleep. But when the officer moved even closer and addressed him by his first name, Collini turned to him. Even sitting down, he still towered a head and a half above the officer. He bent his massive head over him and whispered, 'Go away.'

The young police officer slipped over to the other corner of the minibus, Collini leaned back and closed his eyes again. They said nothing for the rest of the drive, and after that no other police officer tried speaking to the prisoner except in the presence of his lawyer.

Even before the interrogation, the usual investigations had begun. The police did all they could to build up a picture of Collini. He had come to Germany from Italy in the 1950s as a guestworker. He had started as an apprentice at the Mercedes factory in Stuttgart, took and passed his journeyman's exam there, and had then stayed with the firm until his retirement two years ago. The Mercedes personnel file contained hardly any entries on him; the records showed that he was conscientious, reliable and seldom off work sick. Collini was unmarried. He had lived at the same address in Böblingen for thirty-five years, in an apartment block built in the 1950s. He had sometimes been seen with a woman; his neighbours said he was a quiet, friendly man. He had no previous convictions, and was indeed entirely unknown to the Böblingen police. The investigators heard from his former colleagues at work that he always spent his holidays with relatives near Genoa, but the Italian authorities couldn't tell them anything either.

The examining magistrate issued a search warrant for his apartment. Again, the police found nothing there to suggest murderous tendencies. It was the same with their investigations of his finances; his affairs were all in order. A request for official assistance went to the Italian police in an attempt to identify the gun, but there was no indication that it had ever been used to commit a crime before.

Although the investigators followed up every lead, after six months they were still exactly where they had been at the start: they had a victim, they had a killer who confessed to the crime, and that was all. The chief superintendent in charge of the investigations reported to Senior Public Prosecutor Reimers regularly. In the end he could only shrug his shoulders. In view of way the crime had been committed, he said, the motive surely had to be revenge, but he could find no link whatsoever between the victim and the killer; Collini was as shadowy a figure as ever. And when, finally, Collini also declined to be examined by a psychiatrist, so that the latter could give an expert opinion, there were no more leads for further investigations by either the police or the public prosecutor's office.

Senior Public Prosecutor Reimers gave the murder squad as much time as he could. Something surprising did occasionally turn up during investigations, a small detail that explained everything. You had to be patient and keep calm. But in this case nothing changed, everything stayed exactly as it had been from the first. Reimers waited for months before he finally sat down at his desk, read everything through again, wrote his closing comment and then the murder charge. Of course he didn't have to know Collini's motive in order to charge him with murder – if a defendant chooses to say nothing, that's his affair, and no one can force him to talk. But Reimers didn't like loose ends. He wanted to be able to sleep easy at night in the knowledge that he was doing the right thing.

Before he left his office that evening, he placed the files and the murder charge in a wooden 'files box', a table comprising several compartments, which had been invented by the old Prussian administration. The next day they would be collected by an officer and taken away. The murder charge would be stamped, someone would take it to the regional court post room, and it would be given a criminal court reference number. Reimers had done his work, the matter would take its course, and it was now out of his hands. But he felt uneasy on his way home.

The months after the arrest of Collini ran smoothly for Caspar Leinen. He was mentioned several times in the local newspapers, and new clients came along: he was briefed as defence counsel in six trials for drug dealing, one for fraud, one for embezzlement within a company, and a case of violent affray in a bar. Leinen worked meticulously, he was good at questioning witnesses, and he didn't lose a single case during this time. Word was getting around the criminal courts that he was a defence lawyer to be reckoned with.

He visited Collini in remand prison once a week. His client never expressed any wishes and never complained. He was always calm and courteous, but he would not answer any of Leinen's questions about his motive. Although Leinen kept explaining that this was no way to make a sensible case for the defence, Collini either remained mute or, sometimes, said that no one could do anything to change matters now.

Mattinger and Leinen often met in the evening for an hour on the balcony of the old lawyer's chambers, where Mattinger would smoke his cigars and talk about the great criminal trials of the 1970s. Leinen liked listening to him. They never mentioned the Collini case.

CHAPTER 9

Two days after the murder charge had arrived at Leinen's chambers, Johanna called him. She sounded strange as she told him they had to talk, and could he come to Munich. Leinen drove from Berlin to Munich in the old Mercedes that his father had given him. He parked the car outside the Hotel Vier Jahreszeiten on Maximilianstrasse, where the Meyer firm kept two rooms at the front of the building – rooms with the expensive view – permanently booked for its guests.

They met that afternoon at the Munich branch of Meyer Engineering Works. The conference room, the big oval walnut table, the green curtains – he knew them all. As a child, he had often been here with Meyer. He would sit at that table, reading and waiting for the old gentleman to come back and fetch him. Now Johanna was sitting where her grandfather used to sit. He went over to her and kissed her on both cheeks. She was in a grave mood, and didn't look at him. No one touched the biscuits neatly arranged on porcelain plates.

The company lawyer was a small man given to sudden, quick movements; his cufflinks clinked against the tabletop as he talked. After five minutes it was clear to Leinen that there was no point in this meeting. The company lawyer didn't know anything. He said they had even looked through the firm's archives, but had found nothing, not even an invoice from or to any Collini. He kept repeating remarks of the kind that tend to come up in such conversations: 'I'm right with you there,' and, 'We can decide on that close to the time,' and, 'Let's stay in touch.' He had asked Leinen here only because he wanted to know what the defence was planning, and when he realized that Leinen was as baffled as he was, the conversation came to a swift end.

Leinen crossed the street to the hotel. His bag was already in his room. He undressed and went into the bathroom. He took a shower so hot that it hurt, and slowly relaxed. When he came back into the room, naked, Johanna was standing at the window; she must have a spare key. She had drawn one of the curtains back just a little way and was looking out at the street, a shadowy outline against the blue-green sky. In silence he came up behind her, in silence she leaned against him, her hair on his chest. He put his arms round her, and she caressed his hands. It had been snowing outside; the cars went gliding by silently, the roof of a tram was white. After a while he pulled down the zip of her dress, slipped it off her shoulders and undid her bra. On the street below a man carrying his purchases out of a shop opposite slipped, steadied himself before falling, but dropped his bags, and small, orange cardboard boxes fell in the snow. Caspar kissed the back of her neck, her throat was warm; she took his hands and pressed them to her small breasts. She reached round behind herself and began caressing him there. The man in the street picked up his packages and hailed a taxi. Johanna turned round, her lips parted, and Caspar kissed her; her cheeks were wet, he tasted the salt. She took his face in her hands and held it; for a moment they stood still. Then she turned to the window again, arms leaning on the cover of the radiator, and straightened her back. He came into her, saw her shoulder blades, her white skin, the thin film of moisture on her back, and everything was fragile, simultaneous and final.

Much later, tired, their passion spent, they lay on the bed and talked about Philipp, about Rossthal and their summer, until gradually the words died away. In his sleep, Caspar Leinen clenched one hand into a fist, as if trying to hold on to something transient.

He woke early. Johanna was lying on her back, her head in the crook of his elbow, breathing calmly and regularly. Leinen watched her for a long time, then stood up, got dressed in the dark, wrote her a note and quietly closed the door behind him.

The lobby was crowded and noisy; a reps' conference was being held in the hotel.

He went out and boarded a tram. The passengers looked tired, some of them were asleep in their seats, condensation clouded the inside of the windows. He got off at the Tivolistrasse stop, walked across the English Garden and went through the snow to the Kleinhesseloher See. Right in the city centre, not a kilometre from the street, he saw them: little grebes, tufted ducks, common and red-crested pochards, mallards, coots, grey and bar-headed geese, and a flock of carrion crows. In his childhood, his father had taught him about birds. Ravens, he had said, know everything. Leinen swept the snow off a park bench, sat down and watched the birds until the cold had hardened his face and made his shoulders stiff.

In the late afternoon, he called for Johanna at the Munich branch of the Meyer Works. They drove in his car to Rossthal, where they were planning to look through Hans Meyer's private papers in search of answers. Rossthal was only an hour's drive from Munich, or just over an hour, but when they arrived it seemed like another world. The house and grounds lay in the snow, the wintry light was tinged with blue. They drove over the circular forecourt and parked at the foot of the steps going up to the house. Frau Pomerenke, Meyer's last housekeeper, opened the door. She came down the steps, a little unsteadily, and hugged Johanna with tears in her eyes. 'Oh, Caspar,' she added, 'how good to see you home again too.' She had lit a fire in the big hearth, and said there was supper for them in the kitchen, they'd only have to warm it up. Then she withdrew to her own two rooms next to the housekeeping office, and later they heard her TV switched on there.

Johanna and Leinen walked through rooms where the furniture and lamps were shrouded in white dust sheets. The shutters were closed. It was cool and quiet. Only the grandfather clock in the library ticked away; someone was still winding it daily. In the study, light fell through a crack between the curtains and divided the top of the desk into broad strips. This was where Hans Meyer used to read the newspapers every day. They were always ironed first in the kitchen, so that they would stay crisp and the printer's ink wouldn't come off on his hands. The two of them stood in the room, motionless, looking at the desk. Johanna tore herself away from the sight of it first; she put her arms round Leinen and kissed him, and he felt as if she wanted to assure herself that they were alive.

They took the dust sheets off the desk and found its two drawers unlocked, containing nothing but notepaper of various sizes with matching envelopes, a collection of pencils, two old fountain pens, a dictating machine with empty cassettes. On the shelves stood countless files, neatly labelled:

accounts, household records, invitations, business and private correspondence, all filed by years and alphabetically. They sat on the two dark green sofas, leafing through a whole series of photograph albums, also arranged in chronological order. Leinen remembered how Philipp and he used to look at them: family parties, safaris in Africa, hunting in the Austrian mountains. They knew most of the faces in the pictures. Johanna found a cuttings book labelled 'Caspar Leinen'. Hans Meyer had stuck documents sent to him by Leinen as a child into this album: certificates that he had won in the National Youth Games, beginner's and advanced swimming certificates, second place in the boarding schools' downhill skiing championship. Later, Hans Meyer had got his company's legal department to send him the essays and discussions of verdicts that Leinen had written in legal journals. They too were inside that file in their transparent folders. Sometimes Meyer had highlighted a sentence or added a question mark to a paragraph.

After a few hours they felt hungry and went off to the kitchen. There was roast beef, and the new bread that the cook had baked for them, still warm from the oven. They talked quietly, because sounds had a false note to them in the dark. Johanna talked about her marriage. Her husband had been there for her when her parents died, she said, day after day he had sheltered her from loneliness and death. But gradually everyday life had caught up with her. A moment came when she didn't like to see him there at breakfast, she told Leinen; she'd known that would pass off by evening, but at breakfast the next day she didn't like to see him facing her again. She'd put up with that for two years, and then it was no use any more. For some time now they had been living their separate lives, she in London, he in Cambridge. It hadn't worked out as she had expected.

Later, they took the dust sheets off the old grand piano. Johanna played the Blüthner, but it was out of tune and sounded tinny and wrong in the empty house. Still later, they went up to the room that had been hers as a girl. They slept together under mountains of covers, falling asleep slowly, close to one another, feeling the warmth of each other's skin. Shipwrecked sailors on a raft, thought Leinen. And then he realized that they were not 'in love', that was a meaningless concept – this was simply the way they were.

When he woke up, he thought he could hear the barking of the dogs in the morning, as he had in the old days, and the clatter of crockery in the dining room, and for a moment Philipp was there with him. He looked just as he always had at that time of day: pale, his hair untidy, in pyjamas and with his dressing gown unbelted. He had a cigarette in the corner of his mouth; he smiled and waved. Leinen sat on the window seat. It had been snowing again overnight. The snow had settled on the dark model of a crane in front of the orangery,

76

and its beak seemed to be frozen in the ice of the fountain.

On the following morning they went through the attics and the cellars, they searched every folder, they looked in cupboards and chests, but they found nothing to explain what Collini had done. Then Johanna went to his car with him. Before he drove out of the gate to the grounds, he looked back once more. Seen through the melting frost on his rear-view window, Johanna was a blurred shape leaning on one of the white pillars at the entrance, looking up at the bright winter sky.

CHAPTER 10

The 12th Criminal Court – one of the eight courts of first instance in the Berlin regional judiciary where serious felonies were tried – authorized the arraignment of Collini for murder. As usual in major trials, no further evidence was to be heard on that first day, but a psychiatric expert was to attend in order to give an opinion on Collini later. Nor was the list of witnesses particularly long for the next few days: guests at the Hotel Adlon and some of its employees, police officers including those who had interrogated Collini. The forensic pathologist and a ballistics expert were to give their professional opinions, the latter on the murder weapon. The presiding judge thought that she saw the course the trial would take lying clear ahead, and set aside only ten days for the main part of the hearing.

Mattinger appeared on TV news, always saying the same thing: 'The outcome of the trial will be decided in court.' He was a wise, friendly presence onscreen, with his white hair, dark three-piece suit and silver tie. And when the cameras had been switched off he explained to the journalists what was at stake. The press printed stories about Mattinger's trials in the past. One was regarded as legendary: a man's wife had accused him of raping her. There was all the evidence that might have been expected, haematomas on the inside of her thighs, his sperm in her vagina, consistent statements to the police. The man had two previous convictions for actual bodily harm. The presiding judge questioned the wife; he was thorough about it, he spent two hours going over every detail in her statement. Counsel for the public prosecutor's office had no questions. But Mattinger didn't believe the woman. His first question was, 'Would you care to admit that you've been lying?' She said she would not. He began questioning her at eleven in the morning, and the court adjourned for the day at six in the evening. The presiding judge asked defence counsel to come up to the judges' bench, and suggested a favourable deal for the defendant: a lenient sentence in return for a confession. Mattinger raised his voice: 'But don't you see that the woman is rotten to the core?' On the next day of the trial Mattinger asked the same opening question. And on the day after that. In the end the wife spent fifty-seven days on the witness stand, obliged to answer his questions. On the morning of the fifty-eighth day she gave way and admitted that, out of jealousy, she had wanted to see her husband behind bars. The last question was the same as the first: 'Would you care to admit that you've been lying?' This time she nodded. The defendant was acquitted. Either Mattinger couldn't bear injustice, or there was no way he could lose a case. In any event, he never gave up.

These days the old lawyer sat at his desk every night, seeing the lights from the Kurfürstendamm. But now, the night before the first day of the main trial, he felt old. He didn't want to go to bed. His wife had been dead for fifteen years, but all the same he still reached out for her every morning, half asleep, and he almost always woke with a start because she wasn't there. When she died he had sat beside her on the bed. First it was abdominal cancer, then the tumours spread; in the end the doctors said there was no hope left. She hadn't smelled like herself for weeks, too many medicinal drugs, too much morphine. He had sat beside the bed holding her hand, even on that last day when the ECG showed only a flat line. The doctors said she hadn't felt anything. It had been a relief to him when she died, and he was ashamed of that later. He had risen and opened the window. Down in the street outside the hospital, other people were taking their shopping home, walking arm in arm, phoning, quarrelling, talking, laughing. Mattinger had thought he no longer belonged to that world.

Now he lit a cigar and bent over the files again. When he switched off the light at two in the morning, he knew them almost by heart.

Caspar Leinen was also awake that night. He stayed in his chambers until three-thirty in the morning. There were piles of paper all over his desk; he had sorted the files into witness statements, the opinions of experts, police reports, forensic evidence. Leinen was looking for something, although he didn't know what. He had overlooked some small detail. There must be a key somewhere that would explain the murder and put the world back in order. He smoked too much, he felt nervous, and he was afraid. Hans Meyer's chessboard stood on the side table beside his desk, with the old chessmen divided between the stacks of paper, acting as paperweights. Leinen thought of Johanna; four black-and-white pictures from a photo booth were fixed to the shade of his table lamp with sticky tape. She would be in court tomorrow; she wanted to see her grandfather's killer. He looked at the pictures and realized how tired he was. Leinen found his briefcase, but he put only the document with the arraignment into it; he wouldn't need anything else tomorrow. Then he put the white king from the chess set in his trouser pocket, got into his coat, put his robe over his arm and left his office.

The night sky was cloudless; it was cold. He

thought about the fact that tomorrow three legally qualified judges and two lay judges, a public prosecutor, an accessory prosecutor and he himself would be sitting in court to try a man. Eight people leading eight different lives, all with their own wishes, fears and prejudices. They would follow the code of criminal procedure, an old law that determines the course of a trial. Hundreds of books had been written about it; verdicts were quashed if a court failed to observe a single one of its clauses, four hundred of them or more in all. Leinen walked past Mattinger's chambers and looked up at the windows. The old lawyer had said that every trial should be a battle for what was right; that was how the fathers of the laws had intended it. The rules were clear and strict, and only if they were kept could justice be done.

The tarts on the Kurfürstendamm stood in front of the illuminated ads. One of them accosted Leinen; he politely declined her offer and went home through the nocturnal streets of Berlin.

The police officers on duty in the courthouse began doing the rounds of its courtrooms; they had to hang a notice announcing the day's programme there on the door of each one. The notices said who was being tried and when. The officers would need about an hour; the building comprised twelve courtyards, seventeen staircases, and there were about three hundred hearings every day. An officer fixed a single sheet of paper up with a drawing pin beside the tall wooden double doors with the number 500 on them, the doors to the largest courtroom in the building:

'12th Criminal Court – trial of Fabrizio Collini for murder – 9.00 a.m.'

CHAPTER 11

'A coffee, please.' Caspar Leinen hadn't slept much, but he was full of adrenalin and wide awake. He was sitting in Weilers, a café opposite the courthouse. Everyone came in here for home-made cake and open sandwiches. Some said that Weilers was the real central point of the criminal division of the district court. Defence lawyers sat here every day, along with prosecutors, judges and expert witnesses, discussing trials and doing deals.

'Coffee just coming up. Hey, you're early today,' said the waitress, a pretty Turkish girl. Many stories about her were told in Moabit.

Indeed, Leinen was already in the café by eight, an hour before the opening of the trial. The TV stations had set up their cameras on the pavement near the courthouse; outside-broadcast vehicles were parked there, half on the street; cameramen in thick coats and TV reporters in suits too thin for the weather were standing around in the cold. The teams from the main TV channels had permission to film in the courthouse building itself. Weilers was full of journalists trying to look blasé.

A group of young public prosecutors came into the café. Leinen knew some of them from their two-year training period of work experience. There were the usual jokes about rich lawyers and impoverished servants of the state. Leinen found that no one in 'Cap', the Capital Crimes Department of the public prosecutor's office, expected any surprises.

He finished his coffee and got up to leave. One of the public prosecutors clapped him on the shoulder and wished him luck. When he had paid for his coffee at the counter, he crossed the street to the main entrance, showed the officers on duty his pass to the courthouse and was allowed past the long line of visitors and into the central hall of the complex. He still found it overwhelming: the hall was thirty metres high, a veritable cathedral. The stone statues above the stairwell gazed menacingly down, six allegorical figures of Religion, Justice, Belligerence, Tranquillity, Falsehood and Truth. The idea was to make defendants and witnesses feel small, awed by the power of the law. Even the floor tiles all had the letters KCG engraved on them, the insignia of the Königliches Criminal Gericht, the Royal Criminal Court. Leinen took a lift tucked away in the side wing, went up to the first floor and entered Courtroom 500.

Although it was a perfectly normal working day, about a hundred and thirty people sat crammed close together on the spectators' benches. The

85

crush of the press was so great that seats for journalists had to be chosen by lot. They would go away disappointed, for usually nothing ever happened on the first day of a trial like this except that the arraignment was read out.

None the less, all the major newspapers had sent their correspondents; Leinen knew none of their faces. Four camera teams were roaming around the hall, filming anything there was to film: stacks of files, legal books, and of course Fabrizio Collini. He sat in a glass cage behind the defending counsel's bench, and you could hardly see him. These were TV pictures unaccompanied by any commentary.

Dr Reimers, the senior public prosecutor, sat on the window side of the hall, looking at his watch. A thin red folder lay in front of him, containing only the arraignment; nothing else was expected to be dealt with today. It would be a short day in the trial. Next to the public prosecutor, and separated from him by a pane of glass, stood Mattinger, representing the accessory prosecution.

Leinen went to his place, took the document with details of the charge out of his briefcase and placed the white king from Meyer's chess set on the table in front of him. Johanna was the last to arrive, so that she wouldn't have to speak to the press. He could hardly bear to see her on the other side from him in this case.

Just after nine the clerk who would be acting as court reporter, taking down the proceedings, said into her microphone, 'All rise, please.' When all the spectators and those involved in the trial were on their feet, a smaller door behind the judges' bench opened. Leinen knew that it led into a conference room furnished with a long table, chairs, a telephone and a washbasin.

The presiding judge was the first to enter the courtroom. Her left hand had a slight tremor. There were five tall chairs at the judges' bench, and she placed herself in front of the middle one, with a professional judge on each side of her, flanked in turn by the two lay judges. All of them except for the lay judges wore black robes. They stood looking at the camera teams for four or five minutes. 'Well, ladies and gentlemen, I think that's enough. Please leave the court now,' said the presiding judge in a friendly tone. An officer opened the door of the courtroom, two others placed themselves in front of the cameras and spread their arms. 'You heard what the judge said, please leave the court now.' Gradually the courtroom calmed down.

'Is the defendant present?' the presiding judge asked the court reporter, who was over to her right. She too wore a black robe; she was a young woman, and had tied her hair back in a ponytail.

'Yes, your honour,' she said.

'Right, then we can begin.' The presiding judge paused for a moment and drew the microphone close to her. 'I now declare the first session of the 12th Criminal Court in the trial of Herr Fabrizio Collini open. Please sit down.'

After that she established the presence of the others involved in the trial, read out their names and duties, and asked Collini his age, profession and marital status. Finally she turned to the senior public prosecutor and asked him to read the arraignment. Reimers stood to read out the brief text, which lasted hardly fifteen minutes; a murder is quickly described. The presiding judge stated that the district court had allowed the charge of murder to proceed to the main hearing, and told Collini at length about his right to remain silent. The court reporter tapped into her computer: 'The defendant is told about his rights.' Then the presiding judge turned directly to Leinen.

'Counsel for the defence, I'm sure that you have discussed this with your client already. Would the defendant like to say anything?'

Leinen switched on the microphone in front of him, and a small red light showed.

'No, your honour, Herr Collini doesn't want to make any statement at this time.'

'"At this time" – what do you mean? Is the defendant going to make a statement later?'

'We haven't decided yet.'

'Is that what you say yourself, Herr Collini?' the presiding judge asked the defendant. Collini nodded. 'Very well,' she said, raising her eyebrows. 'Then we have nothing else on today's agenda. The trial will continue next Wednesday. All of you who are involved are required to attend. This session is now adjourned.' Placing one hand over the microphone, she added, 'Dr Reimers, Herr Mattinger, Herr Leinen, please would you wait a moment. I'd like a word with you outside this session of the court.'

Leinen turned to Collini and was about to say goodbye, but his client had already risen to his feet and gone over to the police officers. It was almost fifteen minutes before the courtroom was empty. When the three lawyers were on their own with her, the presiding judge said, 'Gentlemen, we all know that this is an unusual trial. The victim was eighty-five, the defendant is sixty-seven. He has no previous convictions and has led a blameless life. In spite of lengthy investigations, no motive has been found.' She looked sternly at Senior Public Prosecutor Reimers, and you couldn't miss hearing criticism of the work of the public prosecutor's office in her voice. 'I want to tell you that I don't like surprises. If the defence, the prosecution or the accessory prosecution have plans for making a plea or statement of some kind, then this is your opportunity to let the court know.'

The judge, Reimers and Mattinger were looking at Leinen. It was clear that they needed to know Collini's motive for the killing, and were waiting for Leinen to put a foot wrong.

'Your honour,' said Leinen, 'as you're aware, all of you have far more experience than I do, and you know that this is my first major brief for the defence. So please forgive me if I ask whether I understand you correctly: are you asking me to tell you at this point how Herr Collini is going to defend himself? As he told you during the session, he prefers to say nothing at this time. Do you want me to tell you more than that now?'

The presiding judge couldn't conceal a smile. Leinen smiled back.

'I can see,' she said, 'that we needn't fear the defendant will not be ably represented. Let's leave it at that for now, then. Have a nice day, and we'll meet again on Wednesday.'

Reimers put his files together, Leinen and Mattinger went to the door of the courtroom. Mattinger laid his hand on Leinen's forearm.

'Well done, Leinen,' he said. 'Now for the press.' He nodded briefly to Leinen and went to the double doors. The photographers' flashlights dazzled them. Mattinger placed himself in front of the cameras. In spite of his tanned skin, he looked pale just now, and Leinen heard him saying again and again, 'Wait for the end of the trial, ladies and gentlemen, and then we'll see. I'm sorry, but I'm not making any comment now. Wait and see.'

Leinen made his way past the reporters.

Johanna was waiting in a taxi outside the court-house. She asked the cabby to take them to Charlottenburg Palace. They looked out of their respective windows, not knowing what to say to each other. It was warm in the sun, but the park behind the palace lay in shade, and there was a chilly wind. An old woman was scattering birdseed on the path; she must have found some left over from winter.

'Crows never beg for food,' he remarked, just for something to say.

They walked side by side for a long time in silence. Johanna's shoes were too thin for the gravel path. The pale blue copper roof of the tea house shone in the sunlight. They heard a voice coming over a loudspeaker on a tourist boat going along the river Spree. The old woman was sitting on a park bench now. She wore red woollen gloves with the fingers cut away. Her bag of birdseed was empty.

Suddenly Johanna stopped and looked at Leinen. For the first time, he noticed a little scar over her right eyebrow. 'I'm cold,' she said. 'Let's go home. I don't have to get back to London until tomorrow.'

Leinen had rented the apartment while he was still training, and he didn't want to move; he had as much space as he needed. Two rooms, a typical old-style Berlin apartment, whitewashed walls, high ceilings, wooden flooring, a small bathroom. There were bookshelves lining almost all the walls, and books everywhere else too; they lay on the floor, the sofa, the chairs, they were piled on the side of the bathtub. Johanna looked at everything. The wooden head of a Buddha stood among the books. There was a rusty spear-point from East Africa on another shelf, and two pencil drawings hung in the corridor: the orchard at Rossthal. A few photographs stood on the window-sill: his father in a green hat, his mother outside the forester's house. A silver-framed photo of half a dozen young men on the steps outside the boarding school; she recognized Caspar and Philipp.

They drank coffee to warm them up. They talked about Johanna's life in London, her friends, the auction house where she worked. After a while she leaned forward over the table. Leinen took her head in his hands as he kissed her, and a plate with bread on it fell on to the tiled floor and broke. Leinen was thinking that tomorrow morning she would be going away, back to London and another life, one he didn't know.

Around five he woke to find the room still dark. Johanna was sitting naked on the floor in front of the balcony door, her legs drawn up, her head resting on her knees. She was crying. He got out of bed and put a blanket round her shoulders.

In the morning he took Johanna to the airport. People were meeting and seeing each other off, people whose childhoods were not being destroyed by any murder trial. Johanna kissed him, checked in, went through security and disappeared behind a blank screen. He was afraid of losing her just as he had lost Philipp. Suddenly everything around him was moving sluggishly. The benches, the floor, the people, the sounds were strange and muted, the lighting was all wrong. A girl with a wheelie case collided with him before he could avoid her. Leinen stood for almost ten minutes in the airport concourse. He saw himself from the outside, as a stranger who had only a tenuous connection to him. After a while he succeeded in folding his hands and, trying to remember the size and shape of his fingers, he gradually came back to life. He went to the toilets, washed his face and looked at his reflection in the mirror until he felt more like himself again.

At the airport news-stand he bought all the papers and read them sitting in his car in the car park. The tabloids featured the trial on the front page. A traffic warden tapped his windscreen and told him he couldn't park there any longer.

CHAPTER 12

For the first five days of the trial, the court heard evidence from witnesses of the crime and statements from expert witnesses. The presiding judge was well prepared. She asked her questions in a thorough, experienced way, and seemed impartial. There were no surprises; the witnesses repeated exactly what they had already told the police. Senior Public Prosecutor Reimers had hardly any questions, but sometimes enlarged on a point.

Mattinger dominated the trial. The forensic pathologist was called as the first expert witness. Mattinger asked Professor Wagenstett about the angles of the gunshots, the entry and exit wounds, the marks left by Collini's shoe, the intervals between kicks, the kicking itself, and got the professor to explain all the details as illustrated by the photographs. Leinen saw that the two lay judges were sickened by the pictures taken at the autopsy, which would surely linger in their memory. Mattinger asked questions in plain language that everyone could understand. Whenever Wagenstett used a technical medical expression, he asked for a translation, and if the forensic pathologist had none, Mattinger got him to describe what he was saying in simple words. After two hours everyone in the courtroom had a mental picture of a brutal thug forcing a defenceless old man to his knees and shooting him in the head from behind. Mattinger had not once raised his voice; he made no sweeping gestures. The old lawyer sat quietly in his place, asked straightforward questions and looked composed. He was relying on the images in the minds of everyone listening.

After five days it seemed that the rest of the trial would be mere routine. The presiding judge continued to be friendly, the court reporter with the ponytail glanced at Leinen with increasing sympathy. The interest of the press flagged; fewer journalists came to the courtroom every day. It was generally agreed in the newspapers that Collini could only be a lunatic. On the sixth day one of the lay judges, both of whom happened to be women, fell ill with a bad attack of flu, and the presiding judge adjourned the trial for ten days.

Leinen realized that he was losing the case. He had spent every evening sitting in his chambers, looking through the files. For the hundredth time, he had read the witness statements, the account of the autopsy, the reports of expert witnesses and the comments of the police detectives. The crime-scene photographs hung on his office walls; he had stared at them daily and found nothing. It was the same today. Around ten in the evening he switched off his desk lamp. He watched his cigarette smoulder and go out in the ashtray, and could smell the singed filter. Mattinger had said he should think; the answers were always somewhere in the files, you just had to read them correctly. But how, Leinen wondered, do you defend a man who doesn't want to defend himself?

It occurred to him that he had forgotten to call his father today and wish him a happy birthday. He looked at the time and dialled the number in the dim light of the room. His father sounded the same as usual; he said he was just cleaning the shotguns, he'd been out in the game preserves all day, clearing the feed troughs.

When Leinen hung up, it was as if he could smell the gun oil. He closed his eyes. Then, suddenly, he jumped up, switched the light on and hurried over to the wall with the crime-scene photos. Page 26, Number 52: 'Weapon: Walther P38', a police officer had written under the photograph. Leinen examined the pistol closely; he picked up a magnifying glass from his desk. He knew that gun. Then he called his father's number again.

Next morning, Leinen went by rail from Berlin to Ludwigsburg. He had found a trail – it was vague and faint, but it was something to follow up. At Ludwigsburg station he asked a taxi driver about the address. The cabby said it wasn't far, he could easily walk it, but of course he'd be happy to drive him there. Inside, the car smelled of thyme and patchouli, a chain with the Eye of Fatima on it hung from the rear-view mirror. The long buildings of the old garrison town were painted yellow and pink, everything here looked neat and tidy. The driver asked Leinen where he had come from, and said that his daughter was studying in Berlin. That was a fine city too, he added, like Ludwigsburg, only bigger. They passed the town hall and the castle, and stopped outside a rather dilapidated building. Leinen got out and crossed the small square. On his left was the gatehouse, an old entrance to the city. Later, gravediggers had lived there, and for a few years it had been an educational institution for delinquent children. The narrow wall of the tall building faced the street; it used to be known to the locals as 'the blockhouse'. It had been a prison for many years, and the prison walls still stood. The government department that Leinen had come to visit had moved there only the year before, in 2000.

Leinen had to shout his name into the intercom a couple of times; it had a loose contact. An automatic buzzer opened the rusty gate in the wall. Leinen crossed the interior courtyard to an iron door. It was unlocked. Inside the place looked as government departments always do: PVC floor covering, neon lighting, woodchip wallpaper, aluminium door handles. There were empty drinks crates outside the lodge at the entrance; the officers in their blue uniforms were friendly and sounded bored. It was all well-worn, slightly shabby, but no one was concerned about that, no one was going to renovate the place. A courteous, lanky man greeted Leinen, took him to the reading room on the first floor and explained the procedure there. Leinen had telephoned in advance. He had hardly anything to go on, just a name and a country. He had thought there was no chance of finding anything out, but the government employees had come up with what he was looking for among the million and a half index cards. Documents lay on the pale wood table, fourteen blue-grey folders, neatly labelled and stacked in a pile. An old woman sitting one chair away from him could hardly see what she was reading; she held a sheet of paper right up to her eyes and moved it from right to left to decipher it. She kept shaking her head, and sometimes she sighed.

After the courteous man had gone away, Leinen, still standing, picked up the first folder. He hesitated to open it. He could see the bus stop from the window. A schoolboy was fooling around there with his girlfriend; they were laughing, messing about, then kissing again. At last Leinen took off his jacket and hung it over the back of his chair. He sat down and took a sheaf of thin, yellowed papers out of the folder.

That evening he took a room in a cheap boarding house near the station. At night he listened to the endless goods trains passing, while the traffic lights outside his window bathed the room by turns in red, amber and green. He stayed in Ludwigsburg for five days. Every morning at eight he walked the short distance back to the reading room. He bought himself a travel guide, and realized that the history of the city was the history of the wars it had known. In 1812, the Württemberg army came here, almost sixteen thousand men, fighting for Napoleon; nearly all of them died in Russia. In the First World War a hundred and twenty-eight officers and four thousand one hundred and sixty men of the Old Württemberg Regiment died 'on the field of honour', as the wording carved in stone on a war memorial said. In 1940 the film *Jew Süss* was made in this city, because the real-life Joseph Süss Oppenheimer had lived in Ludwigsburg.

Leinen sat in the reading room, the stack of folders at his place rising higher every day, his notes filling page after page, notepad after notepad. He asked for so many photocopies that the reading-room staff began to groan. Leinen always worked through until evening, he didn't stop for a break; his eyes were red-rimmed. At first the files seemed strange to him; he hardly understood what he was reading. But gradually all that changed. There in the large, bare room the paper came to life, it all reached out to him, and by night he dreamed of the files. When he drove back to Berlin he had lost all of two kilos in weight. He carried boxes full of photocopies into his chambers, went to his apartment, drew the curtains and lay in bed all weekend. On Monday he visited Collini in remand prison. And when, seven hours later, Leinen left the prison again, he knew what he must do.

CHAPTER 13

On the day before the trial was to continue, Mattinger gave a party to celebrate his sixty-fifth birthday. Leinen arrived late for it; he had been working in his chambers up to the last minute, preparing for the next day in court. He had to park his old car some way off. He passed a long line of expensive vehicles before he reached the gate to Mattinger's property, showed a security man his invitation and went into the courtyard.

Mattinger had invited over eight hundred guests. A large marquee had been put up on the lawn going down to the lake outside the house, a band was playing jazz, there were countless candles in coloured-glass lanterns on the two terraces, in the grass and on the landing stage. Mattinger had hired a large boat that put in there from time to time to take guests out on the lake.

'Good evening, Herr Leinen. Mattinger said that if you were here, this was where I'd probably find you. He obviously knows you very well.'

Leinen turned his head as he sat there. It was Baumann, the company lawyer from the Meyer

101

Works. He was holding a glass, and he wore a dress shirt with a wing collar. Even in the dark, his face still looked red. Leinen stood up to shake hands. Baumann sat down on another wicker seat beside him.

'Nice house Mattinger has,' said Baumann. 'I can't wait to see the firework display on the lake.'

'There's probably too much mist for a good view of it,' said Leinen.

'Yes, maybe. How's the trial going?'

'So-so,' said Leinen. He didn't want to talk about it. He looked out at the black lake again.

'I'd like to make you a proposition,' said Baumann.

'A proposition?'

'It's like this: I don't mind what sentence your client gets. Indeed, I couldn't care less.' Baumann crossed his legs.

'That's certainly the correct attitude.' Leinen didn't like this conversation.

'I'll be perfectly frank, Herr Leinen. We know you've been to Ludwigsburg.'

Leinen looked at him.

'Give up the brief. That's the best thing for you to do,' said Baumann.

Leinen did not reply. He waited to hear more.

'I've been a practising lawyer myself, you see. I know how hard a man works, how ambitious he feels. You stake everything on a case like this, you feel it's the most important thing in the world. If you were just any young lawyer I wouldn't bother, but in a way you're part of the Meyer family, you have a future ahead of you, and . . .'

'And?'

'. . . and you can extricate yourself from this trial without any difficulty. The Meyer Works will pay for a mandated defence counsel, we already have someone in mind who'd do it. Then you'd be automatically released from the case and rid of your brief.' Baumann's voice hadn't changed, it still sounded friendly. The big boat was so close now that you could hear its passengers through the mist. A woman cried out aloud and then laughed. The navigation lights lit up the landing stage, and were reflected in Baumann's glasses.

Baumann leaned forward and placed his hand on Leinen's arm. Now he was talking to him almost as if he were a child. 'Don't you understand, Herr Leinen? I like you, you're just starting out, you have your whole career ahead of you. Don't spoil it all now.'

'Please, Herr Baumann, just enjoy the party. This isn't the place for such a discussion.'

Baumann's voice sounded forced, as if he were speaking under great stress. 'Listen, we don't know what you've been digging up in Ludwigsburg . . . we don't want to know, either. But we're anxious for this trial to come to a swift end. Every day in the glare of publicity is damaging to the company.'

'I can't help that.'

'Yes, you can.' Baumann's breath came noisily.

'Make no plea in court, just let the trial come to an end. Quietly, do you see?'

'Why should I do that?'

'We'd speak to the court ourselves and explain that we'd agree to a lenient sentence.'

'I don't think that has anything to do with it.'

'And in addition we'd pay compensation for your client's cooperation.'

'You'd do what . . .?'

'We'd pay. A considerable sum, to bring the trial to an end quickly.'

It was a moment before Leinen could take it in. His mouth was dry. They had decided to buy a man's past.

'You'd pay me to refrain from defending Collini properly? Do you really mean that seriously?'

'It's the suggestion of the board,' said Baumann.

'Does Johanna Meyer know about this?'

'No, it's a matter between the company and you.'

All this could only mean that they were afraid, thought Leinen. He had got things right, not that knowing it gave him any satisfaction.

'Come on . . .' The beam of a small searchlight on the boat briefly fell on Baumann's red face. 'Look at it this way: you have chambers at the back of a building, your car is fifteen years old, and you're wasting your abilities on small-time drug pushers and brawls in bars. We're on good terms with a bank that happens to have a problem in Düsseldorf at the moment; it looks like being the biggest insider-dealing trial of the post-war era. If you like you can represent one of the defendants. You'd earn good money: the daily rate is 2,500 euros a day, plus additional expenses. The main trial will last a year, at least a hundred days. We'll help you if you like. We can also offer you other briefs. Think about it, Herr Leinen. What you do now will determine the rest of your life . . .'

Baumann went on, but Leinen had stopped listening. The mist was getting thicker, a wind rose. He heard the cry of a mallard in flight overhead, but he couldn't see the bird. He interrupted Baumann. 'I'm not accepting your offer.'

'What?' Baumann wasn't pretending, he was genuinely astonished.

'You don't get it at all,' said Leinen quietly, getting to his feet. 'Goodbye.' He walked over the landing stage and back to the marquee. He heard Baumann call something after him. The large boat on the lake turned, its lights illuminating the bank. A few guests in dinner jackets and evening dresses stood outside the marquee, raising their glasses to the passengers on the boat. There was a smell of diesel fuel and decay.

Leinen passed the marquee and went up the steps to the house. Mattinger was standing in a brightly lit room, his arm round his girlfriend. She was pointing to something or other out on the lake, Mattinger was looking in a different direction. Leinen wondered whether to say goodbye to him, but there were too many people in there for his liking. He went to his car. When he unlocked it, the firework display was going off. He sat on the bonnet of the car smoking, and watched for a while.

The air was musty at home in his apartment. He opened the window, undressed and lay down on his bed. 'A defence lawyer defends his client, no more and no less,' Mattinger had said. That was supposed to help, but it didn't. Then he thought of Johanna, and of the trial of Fabrizio Collini, which wouldn't really begin until tomorrow.

CHAPTER 14

It was the seventh day of the trial. The presiding judge had the resumption of the trial announced, stated for the record that everyone was present, and said she was glad that the lay judge was better again.

'For all involved, I will make the following remark,' she said. 'Counsel for the defence told me yesterday that there would be testimony provided by his client, and as we have nothing else on the agenda today, I would like to hear it now.' She turned to Leinen. 'Is that still how things stand?'

'Yes, your honour.'

'Very well, Herr Leinen, you have the floor.' The presiding judge leaned back.

Leinen drank a sip of water. He looked at Johanna. He had told her on the phone yesterday that today would be terrible for her, but there was no alternative. Leinen stood there, calm and upright at his place in front of the lectern. He began reading, slowly, softly, speaking almost without emphasis. Everyone in the courtroom sensed the young lawyer's concentration as he spoke in his first major trial. Apart from his voice, nothing could be heard in the courtroom except the sound as he turned the pages. He seldom raised his eyes, and when he did he looked at every one of the judges in turn. Leinen used the dry language of the law, saying only what he had heard from Collini and what he had found in the files in Ludwigsburg. But as he read out the statement, as he presented the horror of it sentence by sentence, the courtroom itself changed. People, landscapes and towns came into view, the sentences became images, the images came to life, and much later one of those who had heard Leinen said he had been able to smell the fields and meadows of Collini's childhood. However, something else, something different, was happening to Caspar Leinen himself: for years on end he had listened to his professors, he had learned the law and its interpretation, he had tried to get a good grasp of criminal proceedings – yet only today, only in his own first plea to the court, did he understand that those proceedings were really about something quite different: abused human beings.

'*Ite, missa est* – go in peace.' The priest's voice was rough and friendly.

'*Deo gratias* – thanks be to God,' responded the eleven children in chorus. They stayed put for a moment, not daring to run away yet. Of course the two-hour confirmation class on

108

Sunday after church was always a pain. The old priest could speak well, some of his stories weren't at all bad, but he was strict, and Fabrizio had already felt the force of his cane several times. At last the old man opened the door, laughed, and said, 'Go on, then, off with you.' The children ran along the schoolhouse corridor and out into the cold November day. Fabrizio got on his bicycle. 'See you tomorrow!' he shouted to the others, and pedalled away. He had seventeen kilometres to ride back to his father's farm. Once he was home he'd take this idiotic suit off at once and put on his robber outfit; maybe there'd still be time for him to cycle to the old mill and meet the others.

On that day, 14 November 1943, Fabrizio Collini was nine years old. He was lord and master of one cow, four pigs, eleven chickens and two cats on his family's farm, he was an outstanding military commander, cycle-racing champion and circus artiste. He had already seen a crashed plane and two dead soldiers; he owned a pair of field glasses, a bicycle and a pocketknife with a stag-horn handle. He also had a sister; she was six years older than him, and most of the time he couldn't stand her. But what mattered now was that he was hungry.

Fabrizio took the short cut, the path over the fields. In between the village of Corria and his father's small farm there was a hill, a place to which courting couples resorted at the weekend.

From this hill you had a good view of the area, which was still peaceful. The Allies had landed in Sicily four months ago; Benito Mussolini had been overthrown and taken prisoner. The king asked Marshal Pietro Badoglio to form a military government, and a short time later an armistice came into force between the Allies and the new Italian government. On orders from Adolf Hitler, Mussolini was rescued from a mountain hotel by German paratroopers, and two weeks later he was installed as head of government of the newly founded Italian Social Republic, the 'Repubblica Sociale Italiana', a Fascist government under the protectorate of the German Reich. Fabrizio knew very little about all that. Of course he knew there was a war on, his father's two brothers had fallen three years earlier fighting in the Italian campaign against Greece, but he hardly remembered them. His father had shed tears at the time. War, he said, was madness. Fabrizio remembered the word – folia, 'madness' – not that he understood what it meant, but his father had said it again and again, and Fabrizio realized that it was some-thing terrible. Now the Germans were everywhere in their uniforms. Sometimes family members from Genoa visited the village, they said the Germans were taking everything they needed away from the factories. The men's faces were gloomy, there was whispering about partisans and assassination attempts, and although the grown-ups tried to hide everything from the children, they didn't play cops and robbers any more, they played partisans and Germans. Sometimes Father put on his grey coat and a beret in the evening, kissed his two children on the forehead and left the farm. Fabrizio heard his sister crying on those nights, and when he called for her she came into his room and whispered that Father was a partisan. Their mother had died when Fabrizio was born.

When Fabrizio reached the plateau on top of the hill he stopped for a moment, as usual. He could see his father's farm, the farmhouse and the little barn. He raced downhill. His sister was standing in the doorway when he reached the paving stones of the farmyard. She was still wearing her black dress from church, and she was crying. Fabrizio jumped off his bicycle, which fell over. He ran to her. She hugged him and kept on saying, 'They've taken Father away. The Germans have taken Father away.' Fabrizio began to cry as well. The children stood like that for a long time. Fabrizio had questions to ask, but his sister wouldn't talk to him.

After a while they let go of each other and went into the kitchen. Mechanically, his sister went over to the stove, broke two eggs into a pan and cut bread. Fabrizio ate, she herself didn't touch the food on her plate. 'When you've finished,' she said, 'we'll go to see Uncle Mauro. He's sure to know what to do.' Mauro was their mother's elder brother, a hard man with no children, and their

only living relation. His farm was almost ten kilometres away. Fabrizio's sister stroked his head and
looked out of the window. Suddenly she jumped
up, crying, 'Run, Fabrizio, they're coming back.'
Fabrizio heard the hammering of the engine, he
could see the German military vehicle through the
window, a jeep with the windscreen folded down
and spare tyres on the bonnet. There was a single
soldier at the wheel. 'Run, go on, run!' cried his
sister. The fear in her voice frightened Fabrizio.
He ran across the farmyard and hid in the big dog
kennel that had stood empty for years, where he
rolled himself up in a dirty blanket that was
scratchy and full of holes. Through a crack between
the boards of the kennel he saw the tyres of the
jeep, and a pair of boots that stood still for a
moment, turned and went towards the house.
Then he heard his sister scream. He couldn't help
it, he crawled out of the kennel, ran back to the
farmhouse door and pushed the door of the
kitchen open.

His sister was lying on her back on the wide
kitchen table, her head towards the door. Her
dress was torn, her white underwear spilling out
over its coarse fabric. The man stood between
her legs; he had let his trousers drop, his shirt
and jacket were buttoned up. Fabrizio knew what
the military badge meant, he was a private
soldier, not an officer. He had a huge, jagged
scar on his forehead. He had put his pistol to
the girl's breast, the hammer cocked, his finger on

112

the trigger. She was bleeding from a wound on her forehead; there was hair stuck to the butt of the pistol. The man's face was red, he was panting and sweating.

Fabrizio screamed. It was a loud scream, louder than any other noise in the farmyard, a single high note, and as he screamed everything happened at the same time. The soldier, startled, stepped back. The girl was wearing a gold chain with an enamel locket showing the Virgin Mary, a present from her mother. The sights of the pistol caught in the chain, which stretched taut round the girl's neck, holding the gun in place. The man snatched at the pistol, its resistance was transferred to the trigger. A shot rang out. The bullet went through the girl's neck, tearing through her artery, and emerged to embed itself in the kitchen table. She clutched at her throat, and blood came welling out between her hands. The soldier stumbled back, slipped, and fell on the floor. Fabrizio was still screaming. He couldn't make sense of the images: the pale blue smoke from the shot, the erect penis, the blood on the kitchen table. Then he saw his father's brown tobacco tin. It was standing on the kitchen shelves where it had always stood. Every evening after supper, Father would roll two cigarettes and talk to the children while he smoked them. Fabrizio could see the two Red Indians on the lacquered wooden lid, they were sitting by the campfire, peacefully, eternally. He stopped screaming. The soldier was sitting on the floor with the pistol in his lap. He stared at Fabrizio. The soldier's eyes were like water, pale blue, almost colourless. Fabrizio had never seen eyes like that before; he couldn't look away from them. He simply stood there looking into the man's watery pale eyes. Only when the soldier moved did he manage to move as well, and at last he realized that he must run for his life.

Fabrizio ran out of the kitchen and over the farmyard, slipping on the wet paving stones and hurting his right knee. Father would be angry with him for tearing his Sunday trousers. On past the dog kennel and the pond, into the pine forest, then over the narrow bridge and along the wood-land path until he was out on the open plain. He didn't know how long he had been running, he could have gone on running for ever, but then he saw his uncle's farmhouse. The house was very different from his father's, a large, long house standing on a rise in the ground, with an avenue of pine trees leading up to it. The front door was not locked. Fabrizio almost ran down his Aunt Giulia at the entrance. He stammered breath-lessly until his uncle arrived with the two farm labourers, then he spoke more calmly, and at last his uncle understood. He took his shotgun from the cupboard and drove out of the yard in his car.

When Uncle Mauro came back night had fallen. He sat down on the steps outside the door and stared into the darkness. It had turned cold. Fabrizio went to join him. His uncle opened his huge woollen coat and Fabrizio sat down on its lining beside him. Uncle Mauro put one arm round him. He smelled of smoke, his face and hands were sooty. In the yellow light from the kitchen window, Fabrizio saw wet furrows on his uncle's soot-blackened cheeks.

'Fabrizio, my boy.'

'Yes, Uncle,' he said.

'Your farm has been burned down and your sister is dead.'

'Is she burned too?'

'Yes.'

'All of her?'

'Yes, all of her.'

'Did you see her?'

Uncle Mauro nodded.

'What about the animals? Are the animals burned as well?'

'The cow, yes. I don't know about the others,' said his uncle. 'They may be in the forest by now.'

Fabrizio thought about the animals in the forest. They must be cold and hungry. Particularly the pigs, they were always hungry.

'They can make friends with the wild boar,' said Fabrizio. He saw his uncle's rough hand in front of his face. It wasn't like his father's hands, it was larger, hairier, darker. And it smelled different.

'Your sister told you the soldiers took your father away?'

'Yes, she said it was the Germans.'

'Did she say where to?'

'No,' said Fabrizio.

'I'll go to Genoa in the morning,' said his uncle.

'But why did they take him away? Has he done something wrong?'

'No,' said his uncle. 'He did what was right.' Fabrizio could feel how tense his uncle's muscles were.

'Will you go and fetch him?' he asked after a while.

'We'll see what they say.' He drew Fabrizio closer. 'You'll stay here and live with us now.'

'What about school? Do I have to go to school tomorrow?'

'No,' said his uncle. 'Not tomorrow.'

'Will the animals go to Heaven too?'

'I don't know, my boy. Animals aren't either good or bad.'

They went on sitting there. Uncle Mauro put the coat over Fabrizio's head. The woollen fabric was warm, but itchy on his throat.

Next day Uncle Mauro went to Genoa. He wore his best suit, and Aunt Giulia had packed four trays of eggs for their relations in the city. Fabrizio and Aunt Giulia stood on the steps waving goodbye as he drove away. For the next few days the elder

116

labourer saw to the work around the farm, and the younger one went to the local police station to report what had happened. The chickens came back to the burned-out walls the next day, and the farm labourer found one of the pigs in the forest. The old priest came to see Fabrizio, bringing chocolate, and gave him a rosary with a little silver cross.

Mauro stayed in the city for four days. When he came back he looked tired, his shoes were pinching, the suit hung crooked on his shoulders and was stained. They all sat round the dining table as he smoothed out a piece of paper. He said he hadn't been allowed to see Fabrizio's father, but now he knew where he was. The piece of paper looked official, thin paper marked by two rubber stamps, one top left, one bottom right, showing swastikas. The paper bore the words 'Security Service'. Uncle Mauro said that partisans were very special prisoners of the SS. He read out Fabrizio's father's name slowly, tracing the words on the page with his fingers. After every sentence they all talked at once, trying to make out what it meant. The paper gave the name of the prison; it was in the Marassi district of Genoa. The two farm labourers nodded to each other and hunched their heads down between their shoulders. And finally Uncle Mauro read out that Fabrizio's father had been arrested by order of the security service detachment posted in Milan. He read out the name of the man who was now in charge of the prisoners, a German; Uncle Mauro took a lot of trouble to pronounce it correctly. The piece of paper gave it as SS-Sturmbannführer Hans Meyer.

CHAPTER 15

'SS-Sturmbannführer Hans Meyer,' said Leinen. Several spectators in Courtroom 500 let out a gasp, and there was a commotion on the press bench as a number of reporters stood up to go and phone their newsrooms.

'Hans Meyer,' Leinen repeated, more quietly; it was as if he were talking to himself. He turned to the presiding judge.

'Your honour, if it's all right, I'd like to wait to continue this statement on the next day of the trial. My client is worn out, and . . . and, to be honest, I'm rather tired myself.'

Leinen knew the presiding judge was annoyed. Preparations for this trial had gone on for months, and now it wasn't going to be possible to bring it to a conclusion in the remaining three days set aside for it. Of course defence counsel had a right to ask for an adjournment – but Leinen was glad that the presiding judge didn't let her displeasure show, since she didn't want to prejudice the two lay judges against the defendant.

'Very well, Herr Leinen. It's midday now. May

119

we know how much longer your client's statement will take?'

Leinen could hear the critical note in her voice, of course, but he didn't care about that. 'I'm certainly going to need another two or three days,' he said. He knew that what he said next would be in the papers tomorrow. He had almost been able to sense the change in the atmosphere in the courtroom: Fabrizio Collini was no longer the deranged murderer who had shot a leading industrialist for no reason at all. 'There will be some more surprises, your honour. I have prepared everything.'

The hum of voices on the spectators' benches swelled.

'Then we'll adjourn for today. The trial will continue next Thursday morning at nine in this courtroom. All involved in these proceedings are required to attend. I'll see you then.' The judges and lay judges rose and left the courtroom through a door behind the judges' bench. Senior Public Prosecutor Reimers pushed his chair back, making a good deal of noise about it, and went to the door of the courtroom without speaking to anyone. The police officers opened the door for the spectators and asked them all to leave. It was almost ten minutes before the courtroom was cleared.

Johanna was still sitting, rigid, on the accessory prosecution team's bench opposite him. She was pale, her lips colourless. She looked at Leinen as

120

if she had never seen him before. He stood up and went over to her.

'Get me out of here.' She was whispering, although no one could hear them.

The journalists were waiting outside the court-room. An officer helped them, opening a small door and letting them through; the reporters couldn't follow. Leinen didn't want to go out through the main entrance; he led Johanna down long corridors to the multi-storey car park. The engine of the old Mercedes wouldn't start at the first attempt.

'Where do you want to go?' he asked.

'I don't mind, just away from here.'

He drove through the city to the Schlachtensee. She sat beside him, crying, and there was nothing he could do. He parked the car on a path in the grounds of the lake, and they walked a little way through the wood there.

'Why didn't you say anything before?' she asked.

'I wanted to protect you. You'd have had to tell Mattinger.'

She stopped and took his arm. 'Do you really think all that happened?'

He waited for a while. 'Shall we go down to the lake?' he said. He thought about her question. 'Yes, I think it did happen,' he said at last. He wished he could have said something else.

'Why have you ruined everything?' she asked. 'Your profession is so cruel.'

He didn't reply. He thought of Hans Meyer. He

could almost feel the old man patting his head. As children they used to go fishing with him, and they had fried the trout they caught over a camp-fire and eaten them with nothing but butter and salt. Philipp and he would lie in the grass while Meyer sat on a tree trunk, in gumboots with his trousers rolled up. He remembered the dark green of the trees and the darker green of the stream where they caught the fish. The old man's cigars, the warm smoke, the heat of summer. None of that would feel all right any more. It would never be all right again.

Leinen went down to the bank and skimmed a stone over the lake. It skipped three times before it sank.

'Your grandfather taught me how to do that,' he said, throwing another stone. When he turned round, Johanna had disappeared.

CHAPTER 16

On the next day of the trial, the benches for the press and the spectators were crammed. The presiding judge briefly greeted participants in the trial. Then she nodded in Leinen's direction and said, 'Please go on.'

Leinen rose to his feet. For the last week he had spent his days in the prison and his nights at his desk. He was glad that the moment had come; he could do no more. He had fallen asleep in the taxi taking him to the courthouse, and the driver had to wake him up. He placed his text on the lectern. As he began to read, he knew that today he was going to destroy his childhood, and Johanna would not come back to him. And that none of that was of any relevance.

At eighteen minutes past ten on the evening of 16 May 1944, all fourteen tables in the Café Trento in the narrow Via di Ravecca in Genoa were occupied. All the guests in the café were German soldiers, as usual, and nearly all of them were serving in the marines. The men had unbuttoned the jackets of their uniforms, they were playing cards, some of them were drunk already. The man who put the bag down beside him at the bar wore a lance corporal's uniform. He didn't speak to anyone; he ordered a small glass of beer and drank it standing. He nudged the bag half under the bar with his foot; it wasn't heavy, only a kilogramme. Before coming into the café, he had crushed the ampoule at the end of the little brass tube with a pair of pincers. As he drank his beer, the copper chloride solution in the bag slowly began to corrode the iron wire. He would have at least a quarter of an hour. They had explained the English detonator to him again and again: as soon as the wire was eaten away a spring inside the tube would be released, and a bolt would strike a percussion cap and produce a spark. They couldn't have used German detonators: they were too quick and made a loud hissing noise. The man put his empty glass down on the bar, placed money beside it, and went away. Eighteen minutes later the Plastit W detonated at a speed of 8,750 metres a second, a far more violent explosion than TNT. The pressure wave crushed the body of the man who happened to be standing near the bag and tore another man's lungs apart; they both died instantly. Tables and chairs were hurled through the air, bottles, glasses and ashtrays broke. A splinter of wood entered an NCO's left eye, fourteen other men were injured, they had splintered glass in their faces, their arms and their chests. The café windows shattered, and the door was torn off its hinges and lay on the paving outside.

The interpreter woke at two in the morning. His back hurt because he had been sleeping on the sofa again; he didn't want to wake his wife and children early in their small apartment. It had been like this for weeks, ever since the new German had taken over the Nazi office in Genoa and was running it like a business venture. The new German's name was Hans Meyer. He was supposed to be putting an end to the strikes in this district – local industries were needed for the production of war materiel.

The interpreter lay there for a moment longer. He often thought that he'd rather have stayed in his mountain village above Merano, where he had met his wife at her parents' inn in the summer fourteen years ago. She had smelled of fresh strawberries. She was much more elegant than the girls from his village: even up there in the mountains she wore high heels. Her parents had agreed to the engagement, he had followed her to Genoa, and for a long time all had gone well. But when the war began her father had fallen sick, and they had to sell everything to pay the doctors' bills. He dealt on the black market: food, cigarettes, sometimes a little jewellery. He could have gone on living like that; after all, the war must come to an end some time.

Then his luck changed. The Germans had been

searching the harbour for 'bandits', as they called the partisans. He wasn't a partisan, he had only been selling his stuff, but he fled with the others and hid in a warehouse. A woman partisan was lying across the entrance; he had simply climbed over her. She was bleeding heavily; the ground around her was black. He waited in his hiding place and heard the woman groaning. After a while he didn't hear her any more. He went over and looked at her. Then he felt the barrel of a gun in his back.

The Germans confiscated his bags of food and cigarettes, and took him to their HQ with them. When they found out that he spoke South Tyrolese German, they said he must either go to prison or be an interpreter for them.

The interpreter stood up, took his things off the chair and dressed. Half an hour later he left the apartment. He cycled to the Marassi district of Genoa. The head of Department V – criminal investigation – had told him to be at the prison by quarter to three in the morning at the latest. They hadn't told him what they were going to do. They didn't need to; he'd guessed it long ago. There had been other attempts to assassinate German soldiers before now, but they couldn't meekly accept the bomb in the Café Trento. They would respond; 'uncompromising measures' would be taken. 'Uncompromising': that was the kind of word the Germans liked to use.

He was given the list in Marassi Prison. It was three in the morning. He had to call the numbers beside the list of names out in the corridor. Only the numbers, no names, twenty in all on the list. None of them had had anything to do with the bomb. Then the prisoners were standing outside their cells; a smell of sleep was in the air. The German from Department V stammered when he spoke quietly, but when he raised his voice he didn't stammer any more. The interpreter had to translate. The men were to get dressed; they were being moved; they could leave their things where they were; they would be sent on. That was a mistake: no one sent prisoners' things anywhere these days. The prisoners knew at once that they were going to die today. Finally the German checked the numbers on the cell doors and crossed them off his list.

The prison yard was brightly lit: the floodlights on the walls were switched on. People's faces looked white, as though they were on an over-exposed film. A truck stood in the middle of the yard, with its tarpaulin cover folded back. The prisoners climbed in and sat down on benches. Four men armed with sub-machine guns guarded them. They were not staff at HQ; they were in marine uniforms. No one shouted orders, none of the prisoners resisted. The interpreter and the officer in charge of the marines rode in a jeep. At the prison door Hans Meyer got into the back of the jeep. The interpreter was in front beside the driver. He didn't understand everything the men in the back were saying. Hans Meyer said something about 'Hitler's orders', about 'General Kesselring', about 'reprisals in a ratio of one to ten – ten dead bandits for one dead soldier'. He had been summoned to Florence, said Meyer, in Rome thirty-three German soldiers had been shot by bandits in the Via Rasella. It was all about 'paying the price'. The interpreter had heard of this incident; the Germans had been military police from Bolzano. In reprisals, General Kesselring had three hundred and thirty-five civilians shot in the Ardeatine Caves; they had had nothing to do with the attack on the Germans, and there had been a child among them. 'Otherwise a neat, clean military operation,' said Hans Meyer.

They drove for about an hour, then the road became narrower, and the headlights of the truck stayed right behind them. Once the interpreter saw a deer, rigid and beautiful, eyes like glass.

When they stopped he had lost all sense of direction. Two buses stood at the roadside. There were German marines everywhere, maybe forty of them, barricading the road. The prisoners got out of the truck. The marines tied them together in pairs by their left arms, so that one had to walk forward, the other backwards.

The interpreter stayed with the prisoners, translating the Germans' orders. Then he followed Meyer and the marines into the ravine. He stumbled, grazed the side of his hand on the rock, grabbed hold of the damp moss on the stones. After going round a bend, they stopped at the bottom of the narrow valley. Thin mist clung to the walls of the ravine. A pit lay ahead of them; other prisoners must have dug it, its sides were reinforced with boards. The interpreter couldn't help it, he had to look down.

Suddenly everything happened very fast. Ten marines took up their positions in a row five or six metres from the pit. Five prisoners were led to the pit until they were standing on a wooden plank. They looked into the muzzles of the guns, their eyes were not blindfolded. No explanation, no priest – no one spoke. The officer gave the commands: 'Release safety catch.' 'Take aim.' 'Fire.' Ten shots immediately rang out. The rocks threw back the echo. The men fell backwards into the pit. After that the marines led five more partisans up. In the meantime an older NCO with a pistol climbed down a small ladder into the pit. He was wearing gumboots so as not to soil his leather boots. Down in the pit, he shot two men through the head. The *coup de grâce*. As if there were still any mercy, thought the interpreter.

The partisans on the wooden boards saw their own death coming. Those who had gone before them lay in the dirt below, one on top of another, legs and arms grotesquely distorted, heads split open, blood on their jackets, blood in the muddy puddles. All the same, they didn't resist. The daily bulletin would report, later: 'Reprisal Operation carried out successfully. No incident of note.' Only one of the prisoners did not stick to the prescribed order of events; the man did not look at the soldiers, he looked at the sky and flung his arms high in the air. 'Viva Italia!' he cried. And then again: 'Viva Italia!' His voice sounded unreal. Naked, thought the interpreter. One soldier lost his nerve and fired too soon, a single shot fired into a scream. The interpreter saw the projectile strike the man in the chest, knock him down with his arms still outstretched. Saw the face of the soldier who had shot too soon: very young, little more than a child, his mouth open, the gun still levelled to take aim. That young man would never tell anyone about this day. It wasn't war now, it wasn't battle, contact with the enemy. It was human beings killing other human beings, that was all. The interpreter saw the young man's eyes; maybe he'd still been sitting, until only recently, in school or in a lecture hall. As long as the interpreter lived he would remember it – a moment of truth, but the interpreter didn't know what truth that was.

At last it was over. The marines shovelled earth over the pit where the dead men lay. Finally they heaved a large rock over to mark the spot. No one in the jeep talked on the way back. By the time the interpreter got on his bicycle back in Genoa, the sun was well up. He didn't want to go home, he didn't want to look at his wife and children. He went down to the sea, lay on the beach and looked out at the waves.

In the evening the interpreter got drunk. When he came home he told his wife about that morning in the ravine. They were sitting in the kitchen; his wife stared at him until he had finished his story. Then she stood up and struck him in the face, again and again, until she was exhausted and couldn't hit him any more. They stood like that in the dark for a long time. After a while he switched the light on and gave her the list with the names of the prisoners that he had brought away from the prison with him. His wife read it out loud. The first name was Nicola Collini.

Four days later the news reached the village where the Collinis lived. Uncle Mauro bent over the boy that night and kissed him on the eyes.

'Fabrizio,' he told the sleeping child, 'from now on you are my son.'

CHAPTER 17

'The interpreter,' said Leinen, 'was condemned to death by the Extraordinary Court in Genoa in 1945.' Then he sat down.

The silence in the courtroom was unbearable. Even the presiding judge watched, motionless, as Leinen put his papers together. At last she turned to Reimers, the senior public prosecutor.

'Would the public prosecutor's office like to express any opinion?'

At this question the tension in the courtroom was broken. Reimers waved it away, saying that he would give an opinion only after checking the papers. His voice was barely audible.

The presiding judge looked at Mattinger. 'Counsel for the accessory prosecution, would you like to say anything?'

Mattinger stood up. 'The events described by counsel for the defence are so terrible that I need time. I doubt whether anyone in this courtroom feels differently,' he said. 'But there's one thing I simply don't understand: why did the defendant wait so long before killing Hans Meyer?'

Leinen was about to say that his client would answer that question in writing later. He hadn't noticed Collini moving beside him. The big man got to his feet and looked at Mattinger steadily. Then he said, 'My aunt . . .' It was the first time his deep, soft voice had been heard in the court-room. Leinen looked round at him. 'Please leave this to me,' Collini told him quietly. Then he turned to Mattinger again. 'My uncle died a long time ago. My Aunt Giulia died on 1 May 2001. She could hardly bear it when I went to the country of the German murderers to find work. But to think of me in a German prison as well would have killed her. I had to wait for her death. Only then could I kill Meyer. That is the whole story.' Collini sat down. He was careful about it, he didn't want to make any noise. Mattinger looked at him for a moment, then nodded.

'Your honour,' he said to the presiding judge, 'I would like to wait for the next day of the trial before I make any further statement.'

The presiding judge adjourned the court.

Leinen went to the courthouse car park and collected his car. He drove around the city for a long time. A homeless man was sitting at a cross-roads with a paper cup. In Unter den Linden a teacher was showing his class of school students the monument to Frederick the Great, and then the monument recording the Nazi burning of books in May 1933. A poster of a politician promised economic growth and low taxes. Leinen would have liked to talk to someone, but there was no one around he could have spoken to. He drove to the flea market on the Strasse des 17 Juni and wandered past the stalls. This was where everything ended up when a dead person's apartment was cleared: cutlery, lamps, prints of works of art, combs, glasses, furniture. A young woman was trying on a fur coat; she posed in front of her boyfriend, pouting. A man was selling old magazines, praising their merits as if they were hot off the press. Leinen listened to him for a while, then he went back to his car.

CHAPTER 18

O n the next day of the trial, Mattinger rose to his feet as soon as the presiding judge had greeted them all. He did not look the same as on the two preceding days. The vertical and horizontal lines on his forehead appeared deeper, he seemed to be full of energy and concentrating hard. The presiding judge called on him to speak.

'Ladies and gentlemen on the judges' bench,' he began, 'last time we met to continue this trial, counsel for the defence supplied the motive for the defendant's actions. The defendant's father was shot on the orders of Hans Meyer. Fifty-seven years later, Fabrizio Collini avenges him. Of course it may well be that a motive for killing is honourable. But if the shooting of Fabrizio Collini's father was legally permissible according to the law in force at the time, the motive appears in an entirely different light. For in that case Collini killed a man who did only what was correct in the eyes of the law.'

Mattinger took a deep breath and turned to Leinen. 'Apart from that, it is also one of the duties of an accessory prosecution to protect the victim. And the victim in the case being tried here is not the defendant, he is still Hans Meyer –'

'I don't understand what you are trying to say,' the presiding judge interrupted him.

Mattinger held a sheaf of newspapers up in the air. He raised his voice. 'Counsel for the defence has succeeded in presenting Hans Meyer as a cold-blooded murderer. Every newspaper is writing about the dreadful things he did, I'm sure you've read the reports yourselves.' He threw the papers down on the table in front of him. 'So now we must hear evidence from an expert witness who can tell us whether Hans Meyer really was a murderer. Each strike must be followed by a counter-strike – that's a major tenet of the criminal code. In other words: we can't keep the court bogged down for months with evidence that the shootings really happened, only to discover in the end that they were justified.'

Mattinger took off his reading glasses, leaned on the table and looked at the presiding judge. 'I would therefore ask the court to let me call the director of the Federal Archive in Ludwigsburg as an expert witness. I have asked Dr Schwan to be here today, and she is waiting outside the courtroom.'

'This is most unusual, Herr Mattinger,' said the presiding judge, shaking her head. 'You have not made an application to produce this evidence, nor has the court called Dr Schwan.'

'I'm aware of that,' said Mattinger. 'And I ask for the court's forbearance, but in the interests of the accessory prosecution I had to act quickly.'

The presiding judge looked at the judges sitting to the right and left of her. They both nodded. 'Well, we have not called any other witnesses to give evidence today. If the prosecution and the defence have no objections either, then I will admit Dr Schwan as an expert witness. But I will tell you to your face, Herr Mattinger, this is the only time I will go along with such a performance.'

'Thank you very much,' said Mattinger, sitting down.

The presiding judge asked a police officer to call the expert witness. She entered the courtroom and went over to the witness stand. Hair combed back, not much make-up, an intelligent face. She opened her briefcase and put about ten pale grey document folders on the table in front of her. Then she looked at the presiding judge and smiled briefly.

'Would you please tell us your name and your age in years?' asked the presiding judge.

'My name is Dr Sybille Schwan, and I am thirty-nine years old.'

'And your profession?'

'I am a historian and a lawyer, and at present I am director of the Federal Archive in Ludwigsburg.'

'Are you related to the defendant in any way by blood or by marriage?'

'No.'

'Dr Schwan, the law stipulates that I must advise you of the following points. You must make your report without prejudice, to the best of your knowledge and according to your conscience. You may be asked to swear to that on oath. Perjury carries a penalty of at least a year in prison.' The presiding judge turned to Mattinger. 'Herr Mattinger, you have asked Dr Schwan to attend this court. The court does not know on what subject you want to question the witness, so I authorize you to ask questions directly. Very well, please begin.' The presiding judge leaned back.

'Thank you very much.' Mattinger looked over the top of his reading glasses at the expert witness. 'Dr Schwan, can you tell us something about your education and training?'

'I studied law and medieval history at the University of Bonn. I graduated in both subjects and obtained a doctorate in history. After that I did two years of in-service training at the College of Archivists in Marburg. For the last eighteen months I have been director of the branch office of the Federal Archive in Ludwigsburg.'

'What archive exactly is that?'

'In 1958 the Central Office of Justice Departments of the Federal States was founded to cast light on crimes committed by the National Socialists. There was office space available in Ludwigsburg, and so the Central Office was set up there. Judges and public prosecutors from all the Federal States of Germany were sent there. As far as possible they were to assemble all the documentation still extant on the crimes of the Nazis, carry out preliminary investigations, and then pass proceedings on to the public prosecution offices of the states concerned. On 1 January 2000 a branch office of the Federal Archive was set up in the Ludwigsburg building. We manage documentation from the Central Office. There are about eight hundred to a thousand metres of archival material in the branch office.'

'So as director of the archive you are professionally concerned with the shootings of hostages and partisans in the Third Reich.'

'Yes.'

'Can you explain to the court, in plain language, what the shooting of partisans actually entailed?'

'Both the Germans and the Allies shot civilians during the Second World War. These shootings were viewed as reprisals for attacks on their own fighting forces, and a means of forcing the population not to try any more attacks.'

'I understand. Did that kind of thing happen often?'

'Yes, very often. For instance, thirty thousand people were shot in France alone. In all, the figures run into hundreds of thousands.'

'And did these shootings lead to criminal proceedings after the fall of National Socialism?'

'Yes, in many countries they did. For instance in France, Norway, the Netherlands, Denmark, Austria, before the British military court in Italy, and before the American military court at Nuremberg in immediate post-war Germany. Later, of course, there were also trials in the Federal Republic.'

'With what result?'

'It varied. Some defendants were acquitted, some were found guilty.'

'How did the American military court in Nuremberg see it, for instance?'

'In what was known as the Hostages Trial, a number of German generals were accused of responsibility for the killing of hundreds of thousands of innocent civilians in Greece, Albania and Yugoslavia. The prosecution called for a guilty verdict.'

'And how did the court decide?'

'The court described the killing as a "barbaric relic from the distant past". But . . .'

'But what?' asked Mattinger.

'But in extreme cases, the court ruled, it had been legitimate.'

'Legitimate? The killing of innocent civilians legitimate? In what circumstances could that be so?' asked Mattinger.

'In a whole range of circumstances. For instance, it was never legitimate to kill women and children. The killing itself must not be cruel. No one must be tortured before execution. Serious attempts must always be made to find and capture the real perpetrators of the attacks.'

'Were there other stipulations?'

'Yes. The facts of reprisal shootings must be

made publicly known afterwards. That was the only way to induce the rest of the population to desist from further attacks. A controversial point was deciding in what ratio a shooting could be justified.'

'What do you mean?' asked Mattinger.

'Did you shoot one civilian in reprisal for one dead soldier? Or ten? Or a thousand?' said the expert witness.

'And how was that question answered?'

'Again, in very different ways. There is no hard-and-fast ruling in international law. In 1941 Hitler demanded a ratio of one hundred to be killed in reprisal for one German soldier – that would certainly never have been allowed under international law.'

'What is the highest limit?' asked Mattinger.

'There's no all-purpose answer to that, but in any case it must not be excessive.'

'Thank you very much, Dr Schwan. And now we come to the real subject of these questions. Are you familiar with the Hans Meyer file?'

'Yes, I am.'

'Let's go through it in detail. In 1944, Italian partisans detonate a bomb in a Genoese café. Two German soldiers are killed in the explosion. According to the criteria you have listed, would that be an attack?'

'Yes.'

'After the attack on the café, the security service tried to find the partisans responsible. They could not be tracked down. Would you say that this condition, one of those you mentioned, was met?'

'Yes, I would.'

'On orders from his superiors, Hans Meyer had twenty partisans shot. The ratio was one to ten. Was that too high, or was it legitimate?'

'I can't give you a definitive answer to that, but it would probably have to be regarded as legitimate.'

'But,' said Mattinger, 'the courts forbade the shooting of women and children, am I right?'

'Yes. That was never legitimate. In all these cases, only the perpetrators of an attack were considered guilty.'

'In this case, according to the file, only grown men were killed in reprisal. The youngest was twenty-four years old. Did international law justify that too?'

'Yes.'

'To the best of your knowledge, were the men tortured before execution, in order to get information from them – which of course was also forbidden?'

'No. There is no evidence of that in the file.'

'Was news of the shooting of the partisans made publicly known?' asked Mattinger.

'The file contains reports of it from three local newspapers. That ought to satisfy the basic principles of international law.'

Mattinger turned to the court. 'In other words,

all the criteria that the witness has named were met.' He took off his glasses and put the file in front of him aside. 'Dr Schwan, were any legal proceedings ever taken against Hans Meyer?'

'Yes.'

'Yes?' Mattinger acted as if he were surprised. 'The public prosecutor's office actually investigated Hans Meyer?'

'Yes, the public prosecutor's office in Stuttgart.'

'When was that?'

'From 1968 to 1969.'

'And was Hans Meyer found guilty?'

'No.'

'No? . . . Was he charged?'

'No.'

'Was he even questioned?'

'No.'

'Ah, I see.' Mattinger half turned on his chair to the spectators' and press benches. 'He wasn't even questioned . . . that's interesting. So although the public prosecutor's office in Stuttgart initiated proceedings against Hans Meyer because of these accusations, although there were investigations and a file was drawn up, he was neither charged nor condemned. We have just heard that Hans Meyer fulfilled all the criteria for a legitimate shooting of hostages. Hence my last question, Dr Schwan: what happened to the proceedings against Hans Meyer?'

'They were discontinued.'

'That is so, the proceedings were discontinued,'

said Mattinger. 'On 7 July 1969 the public prosecutor's office in Stuttgart dropped its investigations into Hans Meyer.'

'That's correct.' The expert witness glanced at Leinen as if for support. Almost imperceptibly, he nodded.

'Thank you, Dr Schwan.' Mattinger turned to the court. 'I have no more questions for the witness.' He had won: Hans Meyer was no longer a murderer. Mattinger smiled.

'We will adjourn now for lunch,' said the presiding judge.

Leinen turned to Collini, whose head was bowed. His hands lay heavy in his lap. The big man had been shedding tears.

It had taken Mattinger only two hours to kill Collini's father for the second time.

'It's not over yet,' said Leinen. Collini did not react.

Outside the courtroom, Mattinger was answering questions from the press. Leinen passed him on his way out. There were reporters standing on the pavement, and one of them briefly pursued him, but Leinen ignored the man. He stopped in a side street, let his briefcase drop and leaned back against the wall of a building. He was having trouble getting rid of the cramp in his thigh. Then he walked past a side building of the courthouse complex, making for the little park. He saw a memorial plaque that he had never noticed before on the high brick wall in Wilsnackerstrasse: 'Madness alone was lord of all this land.' It was a line from the Moabit Sonnets of Albrecht Haushofer, who had written the poem in prison before the Nazis shot him in 1945. Leinen went through the entrance in the wall into a tiny park that had once been pressed into use as a cemetery. The city had put up a tall concrete memorial bearing the words: 'They died in combat, in air raid shelters, out in search of the necessities of life, shot through the back of the neck, or by their own hand.' He sat down on a bench. Three hundred people who had died in the final days of the war lay here, an improbable resting place in the middle of the city.

Leinen couldn't imagine what the war had been like. His father had told him about the cold, about sickness and dirt, about soldiers with icicles clinging to them, deprivation, death and fear. He himself had seen countless films, had read books and essays. The Third Reich had been discussed at school in connection with almost every subject; many of his teachers had studied in the 1960s and wanted to do better than their parents. But ultimately it was all just a distant world. Leinen closed his eyes and tried to relax.

When everyone was back in the courtroom just after two in the afternoon, the presiding judge said, 'The court has no questions for the expert witness. Senior public prosecutor, do you have any questions?' Reimers shook his head. She turned to Leinen. 'Counsel for the defence . . .?'

The clock on the wall above the spectators said 2.06. The spectators, the journalists, the judges, the public prosecutor, Mattinger and the expert witness were all looking at Leinen, waiting. Light fell through the tall yellow windows, and was reflected on the presiding judge's glasses. Dust motes hovered in the air. A car horn hooted out in the street.

The presiding judge said, 'Obviously the defence has no questions to ask either. Does anyone want to apply for the expert witness to be put on oath? No? Good. Can the expert witness be discharged?' Reimers and Mattinger nodded. 'Then thank you for appearing at short notice, Dr Schwan, and –'

'Yes, I do still have a few questions,' Leinen interrupted, raising his voice. Mattinger opened his mouth, but said nothing.

'Rather late in the day, Herr Leinen. But go on, please.' The presiding judge was annoyed.

Leinen's voice had changed; there was no softness in it now. 'Dr Schwan, can you tell us who laid charges against Hans Meyer?'

'It was your client, Fabrizio Collini.'

One of the judges raised his head suddenly. No one had known that. Mattinger's face paled.

'When did the public prosecutor's office discontinue its investigation?' asked Leinen.

The expert witness leafed through her files. 'On 7 July 1969. Fabrizio Collini received notice of the decision to discontinue the investigation on 21 July 1969.'

'Just to make it perfectly clear: we are now speaking of the discontinuation of the proceedings about which Herr Mattinger was asking you before we adjourned at midday?'

'Yes.'

'Did the public prosecutor's office in Stuttgart discontinue proceedings against Hans Meyer because the shooting of the partisans was legitimate?'

'No.'

'Really? No?' Leinen raised his voice. It reflected the surprise of everyone in the courtroom. Everyone but him. 'But that is what you have just told us.'

'No, it isn't. Herr Mattinger asked his questions skilfully, so the court may have gained that impression. All I said was that investigations were discontinued. The reason for discontinuing them, however, was entirely different.'

'Entirely different? Did the shooting maybe not take place?'

'It did.'

'Then Hans Meyer was not involved?'

'Hans Meyer was in command.'

'I don't understand. Why were proceedings against him discontinued?'

'It's simple enough . . .' She took her time over answering. Leinen knew that this question touched on her favourite subject. They had discussed it together for hours in Ludwigsburg. 'The statute of limitations had come into force.'

There was restlessness in the courtroom.

'"The statute of limitations"?' repeated Leinen. 'Then there was never any further investigation of Hans Meyer's guilt or innocence?'

'That's right.'

'So if I understand you correctly, my client told the public prosecutor's office the name of the man who had his father shot. Fabrizio Collini did everything that the law of the land required him to do. He laid charges. He said what the evidence was. He trusted the authorities. And then, a year later, he gets a letter, a single sheet of paper saying that proceedings have been discontinued because what happened is now subject to a statute of limitations?'

'Yes. It was subject to the statute of limitations because of a law that came into force on 1 October 1968.'

The journalists had taken their notepads out of their briefcases again and were scribbling busily.

Leinen was still feigning astonishment. 'What? After all, 1968 was the year of the student riots. The country was in a state of emergency. The students held their parents' generation responsible for the Third Reich. And in that of all years – 1968 – the Bundestag decided that such acts were cancelled out by the statute of limitations?'

Mattinger rose; he had pulled himself together again. 'I object. What is this? A criminal trial or a history lecture? This matter has nothing to do with the proceedings of the court. Obviously the Bundestag of the time wanted such crimes to be

148

subject to a statute of limitations. We are not trying the legislators, we are trying the defendant.'

'On the contrary, Herr Mattinger, this matter has a great deal to do with the question of guilt,' said Leinen. There was a steely edge to his voice. 'It does not change the fact that Collini killed a man. But, as you said yourself, there can be a great difference between whether his act was arbitrary or whether it is understandable.'

The presiding judge was slowly turning her fountain pen in her hand. She looked first at Mattinger and then at Leinen. 'I will allow the question,' she said at last. 'It affects the defendant's motive, so it can have a deciding influence on the question of guilt.' Mattinger sat down again; there was no point in complaining about her decision.

'Can you ask that question again?' said Dr Schwan.

'Certainly. But let me phrase it a little differently,' said Leinen. 'Herr Mattinger said just now that in 1968 the Bundestag wanted Nazi crimes to be subject to a statute of limitations. I ask you, as a historian, is that so?'

'No, it's much more complicated than that.'

'More complicated?'

'There was heated debate in Germany in those years. All crimes from the time of the Third Reich had been subject to a statute of limitations since 1960. Except for murder. Murder cases were still to be prosecuted. Then, however, there was a catastrophe.'

'What happened?' Leinen knew the answer, of course, but he had to lead the expert witness through his cross-examination in such a way that everyone would understand what it was all about.

'On 1 October 1968 an inconspicuous little law was passed. It was called the Introductory Act to Administrative Offences. Indeed, the law seemed so unimportant that it wasn't even debated in the Bundestag. None of the parliamentary deputies there realized what it meant. No one saw that it was going to change history.'

'You'll have to explain it to us in a little more detail.'

'The whole thing began with a man called Dr Eduard Dreher. During the Third Reich, Dreher was Head Public Prosecutor at Innsbruck Special Court. We don't know much about him at this time, but what we do know is bad enough. For instance, he called for the death sentence to be passed on a man who had stolen some food. He also wanted it for a woman who had bought a few clothing coupons illegally. Her sentence of thirteen years in prison wasn't enough for Dreher; he had her taken to a Workers' Educational Camp.'

' "Workers' Educational Camp"?'

'Comparable to a concentration camp,' said the expert witness. 'After the capitulation, Dreher initially settled in the Federal Republic to practise law. But in 1951 he was co-opted into the Federal

Ministry of Justice, and his career began to take off. Dreher became head of a section and director of the criminal law department of the ministry.'

'Was Dreher's past known?'

'Yes.'

'But all the same he was appointed?' asked Leinen.

'Yes.'

'What happened to the law?'

'First you have to know that in juridical terminology only the top Nazi leaders were murderers,' said the expert witness. 'All others were regarded as accessories to murder. There were only a few exceptions.'

'So Hitler, Himmler, Heydrich and so forth were the murderers, the others merely rendered assistance?'

'Yes. They were regarded as people who had only received and obeyed orders.'

'But . . . but practically everyone in the Third Reich was only obeying orders,' said Leinen.

'Yes, that's so. Every soldier who obeyed orders, according to this juridical definition, was only an accessory.'

'Then,' asked Leinen, 'if a man in a ministry had organized the transport of Jews to a concentration camp, by that juridical definition he was not a murderer either?'

'That's right. According to the juridical definition, the people who organized such things from their desks were all just accessories. None of them counted as murderers in front of the courts.'

'Apart from the fact that such a proposition strikes me as absurd – did this distinction affect criminal prosecutions?'

'Not at first.'

'But you spoke of a catastrophe,' said Leinen.

'That law devised by Dreher, the Introductory Act to Administrative Offences, changed the timing of the statute of limitations. The legal administration departments of the eleven Federal states, the Bundestag parliamentary deputies and the legal committees all failed to spot it. Only the press revealed the scandal. And once everyone was awake to it, it was too late. To put it in very simple terms, the law meant that certain accessories to murder were now sentenced as if they were accessories to manslaughter instead.'

'Meaning that . . .?'

'Meaning that all of a sudden what they had done was now beyond prosecution. Subject to the statute of limitations. The killers went free. Picture it: at the same time preparations were being made by the public prosecutor's office in Berlin for major proceedings against the head office of Reich Security. When the Introductory Act to Administrative Offences was passed, the public prosecutors might as well pack up their briefs and go home. The officials who had organized the massacres in Poland and the Soviet Union, the men responsible for the deaths of millions of Jews, priests, communists and gypsies could no longer be called to account. Dreher's law was nothing less than an amnesty. A cold-blooded amnesty for just about everyone.'

'But why couldn't the law simply be repealed?'

'It's a basic principle of a constitutional state founded on the rule of law that once a criminal offence is subject to a statute of limitations, that ruling can never be reversed.'

Leinen got to his feet. He went the few steps to the judges' bench and picked up one of the grey volumes of legal commentaries on the table in front of the presiding judge. He held the book out to the expert witness. 'Forgive my asking, is this the same Dreher? Dr Eduard Dreher, author of the most popular commentary on the criminal law? A commentary now to be found on the desks of almost every judge, prosecuting and defending counsel?'

'Exactly,' said the expert witness. 'He was co-author of the "Dreher/Tröndle" commentary.'

Leinen let the book drop back on the judges' table. Then he sat down again.

'Was Dreher called to account?'

'No. To this day it can't be proved beyond all doubt that Dreher himself didn't simply make a mistake. He died, highly esteemed, in 1996.'

'Back to our case,' said Leinen. 'You said that in principle the shooting of partisans was justified, in certain carefully defined circumstances, by the international law in force at that time.

153

How would the courts and the public prosecutor's office have judged Hans Meyer in the 1960s? Would he have been a murderer or an accessory to murder?'

'Of course that is a highly theoretical question. If I look at what Hans Meyer did beside comparable incidents of the same period . . . I think the courts would not have considered the shooting of those partisans cruel.'

'Would it be different today?' asked Leinen.

'The Auschwitz trial of 1963 to 1965 in Frankfurt confronted large parts of the population with the full horror of the past for the first time. But it was not until the end of the 1970s that the mood really changed. That was when the American series *Holocaust* first went out on German television. Every Monday, between ten and fifteen million people watched and discussed the latest episode. Our lives and judgements are not the same now as they were in the 1950s and 1960s.'

'And what would the outcome be now?'

'The partisans were shot where they would fall into a pit on Meyer's orders. They wore no blindfolds. They saw the dead on whom they fell. They had to hear their comrades being shot before them. The journey to their place of execution lasted for hours, and all that time they knew that they were going to die. Shooting them where they would fall into the pit is reminiscent of the mass shootings in concentration camps . . . Yes, I think that the Federal Supreme Court would judge matters differently today: Meyer would be regarded as an accessory to murder.'

'But if I have understood you correctly, even that would not have been any use.'

'Yes, that's so. Meyer's actions were subject to the statute of limitations. Jurisprudence and the law would have protected him.'

'Thank you, Dr Schwan.'

Leinen sat down again. He felt exhausted.

The presiding judge discharged the expert witness without requiring her to take the oath. Then she said, 'We will adjourn for now. In view of the new evidence that has been given, the court will discuss how the schedule should continue. Please keep yourselves free for sessions on Mondays and Thursdays for the next few weeks. The main trial will resume in this courtroom next Thursday. Good day.'

The courtroom slowly emptied. Leinen remained sitting. Collini said nothing for a long time, and Leinen did not want to break his silence. After a while he came back to the present. 'I'm not that good with words, Herr Leinen. I just wanted to say I don't think we have won. At home in Italy we say the dead don't want revenge, it's only the living who want it. I sit in my cell all day, thinking about that.'

'It's a wise saying,' said Leinen.

'Yes, a wise saying,' said the big man. He stood up and shook hands with Leinen.

Collini had to bend to get through the little door

leading to the prison. The usher locked it after him.

Mattinger was waiting outside the courtroom door. He had a cigar in his mouth, and when he saw Leinen he smiled. 'Well done, Leinen, it's quite a while since I was defeated like that. Straight down the line. Congratulations.'

They went down the steps to the main entrance together.

'Tell me, how did you know I was going to call the director of the archive as an expert witness?' asked Mattinger.

'You're right that I did know. In Ludwigsburg Dr Schwan and I found that we saw eye to eye. She called me after you had been in touch with her. I was able to prepare.'

'Excellent. That's the way to win cases. You're probably the most sought-after lawyer in the Federal Republic at this moment. But my dear Leinen, you're wrong all the same.' The old lawyer drew on his cigar and puffed smoke into the air. 'Judges can't decide according to what seems politically correct. If Meyer acted correctly by the standards of the time, we can't blame him for it today.'

They went out through the main entrance.

'I think you're mistaken,' said Leinen, after a while. 'What Meyer did was always cruel, objectively speaking. The fact that judges of the 1950s and 1960s might have decided in his favour doesn't

156

alter that. And if they wouldn't do so today, it just means that we've made progress.'

'That's exactly what I mean, Leinen. It's the zeitgeist. I believe in the laws, and you believe in society. We'll see who turns out to be right in the end.' The old lawyer smiled. 'Anyway, I'm off on holiday now. I don't want to take any further part in this trial.'

Outside the door, Mattinger's chauffeur was waiting by his car. 'Oh, Leinen, did you know that Johanna Meyer fired Baumann, the company lawyer, yesterday? She was outraged when she heard that the idiot had tried to bribe you.'

Mattinger got into his car, the chauffeur closed the door. He lowered the window. 'And if you still want to be a defence lawyer after this trial, Leinen, come and see me. I'd be very happy to take you into partnership.'

The car drove off. Leinen watched it go until it had disappeared in the traffic.

CHAPTER 19

When Leinen woke up it was already light. The time was seven in the morning; the tenth day of the trial would begin in two hours' time. He went into the kitchen in shorts and T-shirt, made coffee and lit a cigarette. He fetched the newspaper from the corridor, put on a coat and sat on the balcony with his coffee cup.

When he entered the courtroom at nearly nine, an officer told him that the trial would not resume until eleven. 'By order of the presiding judge.' Leinen shrugged his shoulders, put his robe and files down at his place and went into Weilers with only his briefcase. The wind was still chilly, but you could sit outside. A journalist came over to his table. He was phoning his editorial office, the resumption of the trial was delayed, he said, no one knew why, he suspected it was some new petition on the part of the defence. Leinen was glad that the man didn't recognize him. He looked at the people going into the courthouse: defendants, witnesses, a class of schoolchildren with their teacher. A taxi driver was arguing with a policeman: could he or couldn't he park outside the main entrance? Leinen ran his hand over the soft leather of the briefcase; it was stained, and torn in two places. His father had given it to him when he'd taken his examinations. Leinen's grandfather had bought it in Paris after the end of the war; it was so expensive that his grandmother had been horrified. But in the end the briefcase had proved its worth. It had come to be almost a part of Grandfather. 'A good briefcase gives you a touch of style,' he always used to say.

Just before eleven Leinen went back into the courtroom. The accessory prosecution bench was empty. Leinen looked round at the glass cage behind him. 'Where's my client?' he asked the officer on duty. The man in the grey-blue uniform shook his head. Leinen was about to ask him what that was supposed to mean when the presiding judge came into the courtroom.

'Good morning,' she said, 'please sit down.' She didn't sound the same as usual today. She waited, still standing, until everyone involved in the proceedings as well as the press and the spectators had quietened down.

'Your honour, my client isn't here yet. He hasn't been brought up. We can't begin,' said Leinen.

'I know,' she told him quietly, almost gently. She turned to the lawyers, officials and spectators in the courtroom. 'The defendant, Fabrizio Collini, took his own life in his cell last night. The forensic pathologist puts his time of death at two-forty.' She waited until everyone had taken it in. 'I therefore have the following decision to announce. The trial of the defendant is discontinued. Costs and necessary expenses will be borne by the state.'

Someone dropped a pen somewhere; it rolled over the floor, the only sound in the room. The court reporter began typing. The presiding judge waited. Then she said, 'Ladies and gentlemen, this session in the 12th Criminal Court is now concluded.' The judges and lay judges rose at almost the same moment and left the courtroom. It all happened very fast. Senior Public Prosecutor Reimers shook his head and wrote something in his file.

The journalists were racing out of the courtroom to call their newspapers, their radio and TV stations. Leinen sat where he was. He looked at the empty chair where Collini had sat; its fabric was wearing thin at the sides. A police officer gave Leinen an envelope with the words 'For defending counsel' written on it. It was still sealed.

'From your client. It was found lying on his table,' said the usher.

Leinen tore the envelope open. It contained only a photograph, a small black-and-white snapshot, brittle and faded, with a jagged white border. The girl in the picture was about twelve years old, she wore a pale blouse and she was looking intently into the camera. Leinen turned it over. On the back a note in his client's clumsy handwriting said, 'This is my sister. Sorry for everything.'

Leinen stood up, passed his hand over the back

of the chair and packed up his things. He left the courthouse through a side entrance and drove home.

Johanna was sitting on the steps outside his building. The collar of her thin coat was turned up and she was holding it together in front. Her hand was white. Leinen sat down beside her.

'Am I all those things too?' she asked. Her lips were quivering.

'You're who you are,' he said.

In the playground in front of the building, two children were squabbling over a green bucket. In a few days' time the weather would be warmer.

In January 2012, a few months after the publication of this novel in the original German, the Federal Minister of Justice appointed a committee to reappraise the mark left on the Ministry of Justice by the Nazi past. This novel constituted one of the points of reference.

APPENDIX

Until 30 September 1968, § 50 of the Federal German Criminal Code ran:

1. If several persons take part in a crime, each of them has committed a punishable offence, without regard to the guilt of any other person.

2. If the law decides that special personal qualities or circumstances call for a more severe or more lenient penalty, or exclude a penalty altogether, that applies only to the offender or accessory to the offence concerned.

Clause 1 No. 6 of the Introductory Act to Administrative Offences came into force on 1 October 1968 (*Federal Law Gazette* I, 503). Thereafter § 50 of the Federal German Criminal Code ran as follows.

3. If several persons take part in a crime, each of them has committed a punishable offence, without regard to the guilt of any other person.

4. If none of the special personal qualities, circumstances or conditions (special distinguishing features) forming grounds for the penal liability of the perpetrator of a crime are present in an accessory to it, then the accessory's penalty is to be mitigated in line with the regulations on the penalty for an attempted crime.

5. If the law decides that special distinguishing features call for a more severe or more lenient penalty, or exclude a penalty altogether, that applies only to the offender or accessory to the offence concerned.

ACKNOWLEDGEMENT

My thanks to Klaus Frings. Without his ideas and his research I could not have written this book.